The Girl Chasing the windmill

In Room with Don Quixote

SHENLANBAI

Table of contents

1.She passed away

It had been a long time since I last visited a night market. The hustle and bustle were beyond imagination, with crowds of people and a constant flow of traffic. Even the famous night markets of Bangkok probably couldn't compare. The sight of the greasy ground instantly made me nauseous, killing my appetite. A few stalls selling ice jelly, boasting "cosmic-level" slogans, were incredibly popular, drawing large crowds. Walking through the street felt like observing the grand spectacle of humanity. Guanghan is just such a city, permeated with an exaggerated atmosphere. Everyone seems to have an inherent flair for the dramatic, even the ice jelly stalls sport banners claiming to be the "universe's first". It's quite amusing when you think about it.

"Peng, long time no see!" a woman's voice called out beside me. I turned to look, thinking, who could this be? She looked familiar, but I couldn't quite place her. Seeing my puzzled expression, she continued, "Don't you remember me? I'm Hu Lei, you used to buy clothes from us all the time."

"Oh, of course I remember you," I responded casually. "You've changed so much."

"Gotten fatter, you mean?" she joked.

"Not at all, you've become a total knockout," I quipped. "Curvy women are the new beauty icons these days."

She laughed so hard her eyes crinkled into slits.

"What have you been up to lately?" I asked.

"After having kids, I started working at an insurance company," she replied.

"That's nice. Do you sell car insurance? My policy is about to expire. Maybe I could help boost your sales," I said.

"Absolutely! I handle both commercial and auto insurance. Let me give you a quote..." She launched into a spiel, words flowing like a torrent - typical of insurance salespeople, I thought, their pitch seemingly endless.

"By the way, have you kept in touch with Lü Xiaoran?" I asked abruptly.

"You didn't know? She passed away six months ago." She hesitated before answering.

It was nearly the May Day holiday, and the weather in Sichuan was unusually hot this year, feeling more like midsummer. Yet at that moment, a chill ran through me. "What happened? I had no idea she had passed away," I asked.

"She suffered from depression and took her own life through carbon monoxide poisoning."

I couldn't hear anything else she said after that. I don't even remember how I made it back to my car. I just sat there, slumped in the seat for what felt like an eternity.

The world around me fell silent, and my mind drifted back to the first time I met Lü Xiaoran...

2.Hi, my name is Lü

Xiaoran.

On my drive home, memories of the past years started flooding back. It was like everything suddenly became clearer, even the little details I'd forgotten popped into my head. It's strange how life works. There were so many times when I thought we'd never cross paths again, but when I heard the bad news about her, I couldn't hold back my tears.

"Hi, I'm Lü Xiaoran." That's the first thing I remember her saying to me. It was around December that year, and I was at a clothing store I frequented, looking to buy some winter long-sleeved tees. Since I'd been to the store many times, the staff were familiar with me. They all greeted me warmly, and the person helping me that day was Hu Lei.

"Hey bro, we just got some new styles in. There are prints, embroidery, you name it. Which color do you like? I'll grab your size," Hu Lei said as she flipped through the clothes on the rack.

At that time, we weren't that close, and she didn't even know my last name. In this line of work, they just call every guy "bro" if they know them a bit, or "handsome" if they don't. After trying on a few shirts, I figured they were alright and went to pay. Out of the corner of my eye, I saw a girl walk into the store, but I didn't pay much attention. She headed straight over to Hu Lei, and they started chatting. It was obvious she wasn't there to shop; she was Hu Lei's friend, and they were discussing where to eat after work.

That's when I got a good look at her. She was about 170 cm tall, maybe 166-168. I'm 175 cm, and she wasn't much shorter than me. It's rare to see tall girls from Sichuan, so she really stood out. They were laughing and chatting, and I just stood there watching them until the cashier reminded me to enter my card PIN. That's when I snapped out of it. It was clear they'd noticed me looking in their direction, and they exchanged glances, giggling, which made me feel super awkward. I quickly finished paying and rushed out of the store. I even snuck a glance back at her from outside. She was wearing something like a business suit, but what stuck with me most was her black stockings. I guessed she worked at a jewelry store. Her face still had some innocence to it, but her heavy makeup made her look more mature than her age. I didn't think too much of it and went on my way.

In the months that followed, I went back to the store a few times, but I never saw her again. Eventually, I forgot about the whole thing. About six months later, I was in a bubble tea shop when I heard someone call out from behind me.

"Hey bro, you're here too? You drink bubble tea?" I turned around and saw Hu Lei and her friend standing behind me in line.

"Yeah, I drink it every now and then," I replied.

"I didn't think guys usually drink this stuff. Are you buying it for your girlfriend?" Hu Lei gave me a strange look.

"Us guys? Girlfriends? Nah, it's just for me," I joked.

"Hey bro, we got some new arrivals again. Come by and check them out sometime."

"You're such a great employee, always promoting wherever you go. I'll come by this weekend. Hey, do you guys like bubble tea too?"

"Bro, what's your name? Let me make you a VIP profile so you can get discounts when you come in, plus birthday gifts and advance notice of promotions." Hu Lei pulled out her phone and a notebook, ready to take down my info. Her friend had already gone to find a seat.

"My name's Wang Peng. You've seen me so many times, and you still don't know my name? You've got no eye for detail," I joked.

"I've heard Qi Mei call you Peng Bro before. Come on, sit down and fill out the form for me," Hu Lei said, pulling me over to the spot her friend had saved.

I was seated right across from her friend, who smiled at me.

"I've got a form here. Do you want to fill it out yourself, or should I write for you?" Hu Lei asked.

"Why fill it out so thoroughly? Name, phone number, and birthday are all you need. Do I have to write down my hobbies too? Favorite movie? First time buying this brand? I don't even remember," I said as I glanced at the form.

"Filling it out won't hurt. The hobbies help us understand our customers better, so we can give you personalized gifts and better service in the future," Hu Lei insisted.

"Fine, just fill in whatever. I probably won't remember it anyway. Is that your friend? Wasn't she at the store that day?" I asked Hu Lei.

"You don't forget things, you've just got selective memory. Can't remember filling out hobbies, but you sure remember the pretty girls," Hu Lei teased with a strange look in her eyes.

I was at a loss for words, feeling my face turn red. That's when her friend spoke for the first time.

"Hi, I'm Lü Xiaoran. That day was my birthday, and we were deciding where to go for dinner."

"Oh, happy birthday," I said without thinking, unsure of what else to say.

I just remember the two of them laughing. I don't even recall how I left after that.

3.It's time to have a beautiful sleep.

I snapped back from my thoughts as I realized I was already home. I locked the car and stepped into the elevator. When I got to my door, I took out a wet wipe from my bag and wiped my face—I didn't want anyone to notice that I had been crying. I opened the door and saw my girlfriend, Chen Yili, sitting in the living room watching TV.

"Are you ready to eat? Everything's ready," she said, gesturing for me to join her for dinner.

I nodded and said, "Sure," then headed straight to the bedroom to change my clothes.

During dinner, I was distracted, barely paying attention. Noticing something was off, Chen Yili softly asked, "What's wrong? You don't seem yourself today."

Forcing a smile, I replied, "It's nothing, probably just tired from work." I didn't want to tell her what had happened today.

"Do you want to rest early? You don't look so good," she said with concern.

"Yeah, maybe later." I kept my head down, poking at my food, feeling no appetite.

After dinner, Chen Yili went to wash the dishes while I
sat on the couch, staring blankly. The familiar opening
tune of the evening news began to play on the TV, and
in a split second, the same old news anchors
appeared. I didn't even let a second pass before I
forcefully turned off the TV with a sharp "click," tossing
the remote onto the table.

I pulled out my phone and opened a locked album. It
was full of pictures of Lü Xiaoran. She loved taking
pictures, and sometimes she'd even send me a few
sexy ones over the years. As I scrolled through the
photos of her posing in different styles, I couldn't help
but find it all ironic. Then, I opened our old WeChat
chat history, guessing that her last post might've been
on the day she ended her life. Sure enough, there was
a photo she posted, along with a caption. In the picture,
she was smiling, lying on what looked like a bed, her
eyes gently closed. The caption read: *It's time to have
a beautiful sleep.*

It looked like she had held the phone up herself and
closed her eyes for the photo. That "beautiful sleep"
turned out to be her last. She was prepared for it.

"What are you looking at?" Chen Yili's voice suddenly
came from behind me, and I quickly locked my phone.

"Nothing, just some design sketches," I said, trying to
sound nonchalant.

Luckily, she didn't press further and went back to
working on her computer. Once she left, I pulled out my
phone again and started going through all of the photos
she had sent me over the years. I scrolled back further

and further, wanting to start from the very first picture. Since I never deleted our chat history, I realized we had met before WeChat existed, so I opened up QQ to look at our older messages.

The first picture I found was of her in the same work outfit she wore the day we first met. The background looked like a café. Immediately, I was transported back to that memory.

That was probably our first time meeting alone. After exchanging numbers at the bubble tea shop, we started messaging each other frequently within about a week. At the time, I didn't have a girlfriend, and honestly, I liked her. But there was always something a bit mysterious about her. Her responses in our chats seemed far more mature than her age, and naturally, I tried to appear even more mature.

So, we kept chatting back and forth on QQ, and eventually, we agreed to meet for drinks one weekend. She said Saturday afternoon worked for her because she worked shifts at a jewelry store. She didn't have weekends off, but she finished at 2 PM on Saturdays and didn't have to be back until the next morning. We decided to meet at a café nearby.

When we sat down, we picked up our conversation from QQ, and I started to learn more about her. She told me she had started working when she was 15, right after middle school. Her first job was at a cosmetics store, and later she worked at a big local restaurant before bouncing around various jobs. Throughout our conversation, she spoke in a big-sister tone, even though I was six years older than her. But that didn't really matter; I felt a real connection with her, and it seemed like she was open to something more as well.

Since I was an interior designer, we talked about professional stuff, and I was impressed by how much she knew. At least she wasn't talking nonsense.

"You seem to know quite a bit, even about CAD," I remarked.

"I went to a vocational school for a while. My major was computers. I learned some CAD, and I'm also good with basic Office programs. Back at the cosmetics store, I was the one who made the inventory spreadsheets," she said proudly.

"Wow! You even made those spreadsheets? That's impressive!" I said.

"Well, the boss gave me a template, but no one else could figure out how to use the computer, so I ended up doing all the data entry," she laughed.

"Pfft... I thought you were some kind of expert. Entering data isn't that hard," I teased.

"I'll smack you! I was the only one in the entire store who could do it," she playfully pretended to be upset, laughing.

As we chatted, her phone rang. She glanced at the screen, then at me, looking like she wanted to say something but hesitated. Finally, she answered the call: "Hey, Zhao."

"I'm at the Xifu Café on Nanjing Road. Uh-huh… with a friend. Are you coming over? Oh… alright, give me a call tonight." She hung up and turned to me. "That was my former boss from the restaurant. Also, my ex."

4.If you keep acting weird, I'm going to smack that weirdness out of you.

I shifted my gaze from the photo back to the chat we had after that café meeting.

Lü: Why didn't you reply to my message?
Me: Oh, I was busy, didn't really notice.
Lü: You feel different now.
Me: What's different?
Lü: Women have sharp intuition, you know? When we left in the afternoon, I could tell something was off with you. Is it because of my ex?

That was pretty much the conversation. It was obvious that I found it a bit strange—why did she still seem so close with her ex? Her explanation was that after so much time together, there were still unresolved things between them.

Over the next few times we met, it always felt like she was constantly on her phone, either texting or taking calls. She seemed busy, yet at the same time acted calm, like she really enjoyed listening to me talk. We weren't exactly in a relationship—it was more like a mutual flirtation. Our chats included phrases like "I miss you," but our relationship wasn't that intimate.

In the weeks that followed, I decided to dig into her background through some social connections. In a small city, that wasn't too hard to do. She was from a nearby town, from a working-class family—nothing too poor, just average. Her parents weren't well-educated, so they couldn't offer much constructive advice. After leaving school, she worked at a small cosmetics wholesale store, and a few months later, through a friend's recommendation, she moved on to a large local restaurant called "Oriental Pavilion." The place had a rising reputation and was rumored to be run by a mob boss who opened it for his wife. Thanks to these connections, the restaurant's business was booming. While working there, Lü Xiaoran caught the boss's eye and eventually became his mistress.

I asked her directly, "Why would you do that? He's so much older than you. What could you two possibly talk about?"

She replied, "I don't know. He was really nice to me back then. I didn't understand much at the time. I just felt happy, so I went along with it. Later, I realized it wasn't right and stopped contacting him, even moved to other jobs. But he kept finding excuses to see me, not to do much, just to have tea or sing. I didn't know how to reject him."

I knew exactly what had happened. She had just started working, didn't know much about the world, and when a well-connected guy showed her attention, it was easy for her to fall for it. But this changed my feelings. I still liked her, but part of me felt twisted inside, seeing her as less "pure" and wanting to distance myself. I started to ignore her on purpose, which only made her anxious. She kept texting me non-stop. I became a little arrogant during that time. Hu Yao even asked me why I wasn't responding to her, saying that Lü Xiaoran was really sad, that she had even cried a few times. She told me Lü Xiaoran had broken up with Zhao a long time ago and really liked me.

Even when we did meet, I started using harsher words to provoke her.

One afternoon, we met at a café that was known for its privacy. Every booth had curtains, so unless a waiter came in, no one would disturb you. It was a spot where couples usually went. The booths weren't soundproof, and you couldn't get away with anything too extreme, but it was still private enough.

"What's your deal? If you keep acting weird, I'm going to smack that weirdness out of you," she said, breaking the silence.

"Excuse me," a waiter's voice interrupted from outside the curtain. The waiter came in, placed our order on the table, and said, "Enjoy. If you need anything, press the red button on the table." We both nodded, and the waiter left.

"Okay, spill it. What's up with you acting all strange?" Lü Xiaoran continued.

"I'm not acting strange. How am I being weird?" I said, playing innocent.

"Then why do you barely reply to my messages?"

"I did reply! I replied to every one," I said, brushing it off.

She immediately pulled out her phone, opened QQ, and started scrolling through the messages. "Look at this! I sent you so many, and you barely replied to any. Not even a tenth of them!"

"You're really counting them? Sometimes I'm busy and don't see them."

"I know you're bothered by the thing with Zhao. But we're really done," she said, sounding hurt.

"How do I know? How can you prove it?" I asked, with a mischievous grin.

"Prove it? I'll smack you!" She pretended to slap me but ended up with me grabbing her arm and pulling her onto me. I held her tight and lay back, so she ended up lying on top of me.

"You're so bad! I'll find that weirdness of yours and smack it right out," she said, blushing.

Seeing the moment was right, I slid my hand to her butt, and she immediately squirmed, trying to get away.

"Don't do that! It tickles," she said, shifting uncomfortably as she tried to get up.

"Come on, tell me, did you and Zhao ever cuddle like this?" I teased, holding her tighter and preventing her from getting up.

"We didn't. We didn't cuddle like this," she said matter-of-factly.

I wasn't expecting her to be so blunt, and it only fed my twisted curiosity. "So how did you two usually cuddle? What position did you use when you had sex?" I asked, continuing with the teasing tone.

5.Sure, just the two of us?

She froze for a few seconds without answering, still trying to get up. I kept pressing, "Tell me, and I'll let go."

"Well... we didn't do much. I'd just lie face down with my butt up," she whispered.

Hearing that, I couldn't help but have a reaction, feeling a bit embarrassed. I let go of her, but she seemed to notice it and didn't get up. She stayed lying on top of me, making the atmosphere even more delicate.

She slowly spoke, "We didn't stay together for long. His wife found out, and that was it. I quit the job right after."

"Did someone talk bad about you behind your back? Did Zhao really let you leave so easily?" I asked while tightening my grip around her.

She squirmed a little, trying to get out of my hold, then continued, "Whether he wanted me to stay or not didn't matter. I found out he had other girlfriends too."

"Can his body handle all that?" I teased, pressing down on her butt, causing it to press against me.

She used more force to pull away from my hands and sat up on me, lightly bouncing on my stomach.

"Ow," I winced in pain, not expecting her to do that.

"Aren't you acting all weird? Let's see how weird you'll act now," she said while bouncing lightly again.

Her sudden move caught me off guard, and I grabbed her, holding her down to stop her from jumping.

She tried to wiggle free and started bouncing again, saying, "Are you still acting weird? Are you still going to ignore my messages?"

At that moment, Chen Yili's voice pulled me out of my thoughts. "Wang Peng, why are you still sitting there? Didn't you say you weren't feeling well? Maybe you should rest early."

I muttered a response, realizing I had been sitting there for almost an hour and a half, lost in my memories. Everything felt so vivid, like it had just happened. I quickly turned off my phone and went to take a shower. As the water flowed down over me, my thoughts drifted back to that time again.

From that point on, our relationship grew much closer, but in public, I pretended it wasn't that serious. After all, Zhao still called her from time to time, and living in a small city like Guanghan, where shady characters had influence, I didn't want any trouble. If her relationship with Zhao wasn't really over like she claimed, would I end up like those guys in the movies who get hunted down for messing with a gangster's woman? It was unlikely, but the thought always crossed my mind. She probably understood, too, because she never mentioned it.

We continued our routine—working during the day, meeting up for dinner at night whenever we had time. At this point, we still hadn't slept together, even though I'd dropped hints about it. In my mind, it should've been easy, especially after how close we got at the café that one time. But weeks had passed, and nothing had happened.

I finally asked her directly, "How about we go sing some karaoke tonight?" I figured we could get a private room at a KTV, have some drinks, and it would be easy from there.

"Sure, just the two of us?" she asked.

"Who else? You want to invite Zhao?"

"Are you itching for a beating again? Should I smack that weirdness out of you?" she joked, pretending to be mad.

"Hmm, let me think... Okay, I could invite a friend. He works at the quality inspection bureau," I thought of Li Sen, who I hung out with a lot at the time. I had told him I was seeing someone.

"Then I'll invite Hu Yao," she said with a playful smile.

"Her? Hmm... sure, I guess," I replied, a little surprised.

"What? You don't want her to come?" she asked, staring at me intensely.

"No, no, it's fine. I'll let my friend know. Let's go to the KTV on Yueyang Road." I pulled out my phone and called Li Sen.

Within an hour, the four of us met up at the KTV. After the usual introductions, we settled in. Of course, I already knew everyone. Li Sen, being his usual outgoing self, quickly hit it off with Hu Yao, and they chatted non-stop.

"You sure they just met today? They're hitting it off pretty fast," I whispered to Lü Xiaoran as Li Sen sang.

"Isn't that what you call love at first sight?" Lü Xiaoran teased with a grin.

"Pfft, love at first sight? Li Sen's been married for three years," I muttered, rolling my eyes.

Lü Xiaoran glanced at Li Sen and Hu Yao, then turned back to me, saying, "Well, Hu Yao's single, so you'd better make sure she knows that."

Just then, Lü Xiaoran's phone rang. She glanced at it and answered, "Zhao? I'm out singing with Hu Yao and some friends. Uh-huh... uh-huh... you want to come? Well, there are two other people here you don't know... Oh, alright. Yeah, come by, we're at the KTV on Yueyang Road." She hung up and turned to us, "Zhao's coming."

The room suddenly fell quiet.

6.It's fine, he'll probably stay for half an hour and then leave.

Bang... bang... bang... A few knocks on the door startled me.

"What are you doing in there? You've been in there forever!" Chen Yili shouted from outside.

"I'm done, coming out now," I responded.

"I thought you passed out in there! It's been so long. You've used up all the hot water. Now I have to wait another 30 minutes for the water to heat up. I wanted to take a shower early, too, but now I have to wait," she grumbled as I dried off and got ready to put on my pajamas.

I checked the time, realizing how long I had been lost in my memories. I suddenly remembered something and rushed to my desk. My computer and work desk are all in one place, with several drawers filled with old electronics—wired headphones, various charging cables, and some old phones that were no longer in use. After rummaging around for a while, I found an iPhone 4. It was the phone I had used that night at the KTV.

There was a noticeable dent in the bottom right corner of the phone, from when I dropped it that night. But nothing serious had happened—just me slipping and falling. I kept searching for the iPhone 4's charging cable, eager to see the photos from that night. The phone was slightly swollen, and I wasn't sure if it would still work.

I eventually found the cable, plugged it in, and the screen showed the charging symbol. A few moments later, the familiar Apple logo appeared, and the phone booted up. I quickly connected it to the charger and tried to operate it, but the touch screen wasn't very responsive. I figured the phone must have gotten damp after all these years, so I stood up to find some wet wipes to clean the screen.

In the other room, Chen Yili was furiously typing away at her computer, the sound of her keyboard clattering non-stop. She's a data analyst, and her daily task involves entering lots of data into the computer for various analyses. Sometimes, she works late into the night, so she uses the farthest room from me to avoid disturbing me.

She was so focused on her work that she didn't notice me walk in. I gently tapped her on the back and asked, "Do you have a wet wipe? I need to clean my phone screen."

Without saying a word, she pointed to the dresser behind her. I walked over and easily found the wet wipes on top.

"Got a new task?" I asked.

"Yep, the old witch wants our team to submit the results by tomorrow. I just got the email, and everyone's complaining about it in the group chat. She never gives us a heads-up. No idea how long I'll be stuck working tonight," she said through gritted teeth, sounding like a student who waited until the last day of summer vacation to do their homework, only to realize school starts tomorrow and the work's only half done.

"No one dares to stand up to the old witch? It's pretty late to be adding all this work," I said, trying to comfort her. The "old witch" was her boss.

"Just wait till I get my year-end bonus, and I'm out," she said with determination.

I didn't respond and quietly left the room. She's been saying she'll quit after getting her bonus for years, but she never follows through. Meanwhile, I was reassured that she was busy and wouldn't be bothering me for a while.

Back at my desk, I wiped the phone screen with the alcohol wipes, and sure enough, it worked perfectly. I quickly opened the photo gallery, and a flood of pictures appeared. I scrolled back to 2010, the year I met Lü Xiaoran. It didn't take much effort to find the photos from that night, as I vividly remembered that we had taken a lot of pictures—our first group photos, in fact.

In the pictures, there were Hu Yao, Li Sen, Lü Xiaoran, and me. The four of us sat in the dim, colorful lights of the KTV. Everyone's smiles looked so genuine in the photos, making me feel nostalgic, yet everything had changed since then. The memories pulled me back to that night.

After Lü Xiaoran took Zhao's call and said he was coming, I immediately wanted to leave.

"I think I'll head out," I said.

"Don't worry, he'll probably stay for half an hour and then leave," Lü Xiaoran reassured me.

"Who's coming?" Li Sen asked, confused.

"Her boyfriend," I said, pointing to Lü Xiaoran, my tone stiff.

"Boyfriend?" Li Sen was clearly baffled.

"No, don't listen to him," Lü Xiaoran said, visibly anxious.

"You..." Li Sen trailed off, looking at me like he wanted to say more. I hadn't told him the details. He only knew that Lü Xiaoran was my new girlfriend.

I raised my glass and said, "Let's have a drink, everyone. Cheers. I think I'll head out; this just isn't for me."

"If you leave, I'll have to go too," Li Sen chimed in.

"Don't! Zhao won't say anything. He usually leaves quickly anyway," Hu Yao finally spoke up. "Convince him to stay. We haven't been here long, it's still early," she said, tugging on Li Sen's arm.

In my head, I was thinking, *Are they trying to stop me from leaving, or do they just not want Li Sen to go?* I got up, not planning to waste any more words, and headed straight for the door.

As I opened the door, a skinny, short, middle-aged man almost walked right into me. I realized immediately—it must be Zhao.

7.Hey, look at those two.

When Zhao came in, everyone instinctively stood up, and he gently pushed me back inside.

"Zhao, I was just about to leave," I quickly said.

"Leave? No way. Sit down and have a drink," his voice was deep and carried a hint of authority.

The way he said it made me feel uneasy, and I realized that leaving wasn't an option anymore. Truthfully, I was scared. The reason I wanted to leave earlier was because I was afraid something might happen, and I wouldn't be able to handle it.

Zhao was a well-known figure in the area, someone who had influence both legally and in the underworld. I'd never met him before, but his reputation was widespread.

Zhao smoothly picked up his glass, "Alright, let's all have a drink together."

We all raised our glasses and drank in silence.

"Is that the legendary Zhao?" Li Sen whispered to me.

I nodded without saying anything. Meanwhile, Zhao continued, "Xiaoran told me she was hanging out with some friends for drinks, so of course, I had to come join. I love hanging out with you young people. I may look mature, but I'm actually a '90s kid."

As soon as he said that, I nearly choked on my drink, and everyone looked at him in disbelief.

"I started working in the '90s, haha," Zhao said with a bit of a sharp tone to his voice.

His joke left us all pausing for a few seconds before we awkwardly laughed along. Zhao followed the usual drinking etiquette, making his way around the table to drink with each of us as a sign of respect.

When he got to me, he said, "Xiaoran mentioned you're her new friend, so let's have a drink together."

He casually placed his hand on Lü Xiaoran's back as he spoke, which made me feel extremely uncomfortable. It seemed intentional, but I didn't dare say anything.

After making his rounds, Zhao sang an old Cantonese song loudly. Strangely enough, even though people his age usually sang those songs out of tune, he hit all the notes perfectly.

Meanwhile, Li Sen and Hu Yao had already started whispering and getting close to each other. *What the hell?* I thought. It felt like I'd played matchmaker for them. I wasn't even sure if Li Sen had told Hu Yao that he was married, but maybe she didn't care.

After Zhao finished his song, he stayed for another ten minutes or so before stepping out to take a call. I assumed he'd come back, but Lü Xiaoran told us he wasn't returning; he had already left.

"He really only stayed for half an hour. Pretty punctual," I joked.

"His driver waits for him outside. He never stays for more than an hour, for safety reasons," Lü Xiaoran explained.

"Is he starring in a movie? Does he think someone's out to kill him or something? What a nutjob," I muttered.

"Alright, he's gone now. We can enjoy ourselves. Hey, look at those two," Lü Xiaoran said, pointing at Li Sen and Hu Yao.

Unbelievably, the two of them were now kissing. I sighed and turned back to Lü Xiaoran, signaling her to sing and ignore them.

She selected the song "Moonlight in the City" and started singing. It was fitting—a flashy city illuminated by gentle moonlight.

Meanwhile, my hands started wandering up and down Lü Xiaoran's back. At first, she kept dodging, which annoyed me. I muttered, "He can touch you, but I can't?"

Hearing this, she seemed to change somehow— though I wasn't sure how—and stopped resisting my touch. Naturally, I took the opportunity to explore more boldly. When I squeezed her chest, she let out a yelp into the microphone, which made the other two stop and look our way.

I didn't care anymore. I pulled Lü Xiaoran into my lap. The music from the song continued, and the two of them went back to their own business, ignoring what was happening with us.

With her in my arms, I leaned in and kissed her. *If Li Sen's going that far, I can't be outdone.* Lü Xiaoran didn't resist, and the kiss was sweet. Even now, I still reminisce about how it felt.

A few minutes later, I got up to go to the bathroom, but I accidentally slipped on something and fell. Everyone rushed over to help me up, asking if I'd hurt myself. I was more embarrassed than anything and found a small stain on my clothes. My phone, however, had flown a few meters away and hit the floor, which is probably when the dent on the back was made. Luckily, it still worked.

We kept hanging out until midnight, finally deciding to leave, though we didn't really want the night to end. As we headed to pay, we were told that Zhao had already taken care of the bill.

"He's still got some class," I said, half-jokingly.

"Let's grab a bite to eat. There's a noodle shop nearby with barbecue and cold dishes," Li Sen suggested.

We all nodded and headed over.

Everyone ordered something to eat, and Li Sen and I went to the counter to order some stewed dishes.

"Hey, miss, give me 20 yuan worth of fatty intestine and beef. Heat it up in the microwave," Li Sen said loudly to the young woman at the counter. Then he turned to me, "So, what's your plan for tonight? You don't have work tomorrow, right?"

"Why, you got plans? You sure you're going home?" I asked curiously.

"Not tonight, for sure. No rush, I'm just wondering about you two. Seems like your relationship's a little more complicated," Li Sen replied with a knowing look.

With that, we returned to the table. The noodles arrived quickly, and the girls were already eating by the time we sat down. Li Sen and I grabbed our bowls and joined in.

I leaned over to whisper something I'd been holding back for a while, likely fueled by the alcohol, "Xiaoran, let's not go home tonight. Just the two of us.

8.Do you often take girls to hotels?

The phone started heating up as it charged, and I quickly unplugged it, afraid the old device might suddenly spark or catch fire. The screen was still displaying the photo of the four of us sitting on the KTV couch. Lü Xiaoran was wearing a loose white T-shirt and a fitted skirt, with her shoulder-length hair casually draped over her shoulders. She was leaning her head against my shoulder, flashing a V sign with her fingers. Her hand conveniently blocked half of my face. Li Sen and Hu Yao were sitting apart in the photo. The order from left to right was: Hu Yao, Lü Xiaoran, me, and Li Sen. It seemed like Li Sen and Hu Yao weren't quite familiar with each other when the photo was taken.

I looked at Lü Xiaoran's face again. Even though the photo quality wasn't great, and the lighting was dim, everyone's face was illuminated by the colorful KTV lights. Lü Xiaoran had a playful pout, and in that moment, it felt like my throat was blocked. Her smile was so innocent and pure. Tears welled up in my eyes again as I realized I still hadn't accepted that she was gone. My heart was screaming silently.

Suddenly, the phone's screen went dark. I pressed the home button and tapped the screen, but there was no response. Damn it, the battery's dead again. Plugging it back in might let me use it for a few more minutes, but without the cable, it wouldn't last long. I reluctantly plugged it in again, and after a few minutes, the phone rebooted. I didn't care if the battery overheated at this point. All I wanted was to retrieve the photos.

I decided to transfer the pictures to my new iPhone. Luckily, even an old iPhone like this one could still use AirDrop. However, the progress bar moved slowly, and I wasn't sure why. It should've been faster. I didn't dare touch any other buttons and just waited, letting my mind drift back to the memories.

That night, when I asked Lü Xiaoran if she wasn't going home, she didn't respond and silently continued eating. I knew what that meant—she had already agreed.

Li Sen and Hu Yao kept chatting nonstop. They seemed to find endless topics, even managing to discover mutual acquaintances and turning them into full-blown discussions. I was genuinely impressed.

"Li Sen, your team came to our store for an inspection last time. It was a total scramble," Hu Yao said.

"What? Were you guys selling faulty products? I doubt it. We haven't done any inspections in the past year unless there was a complaint to investigate," Li Sen said, surprised.

"That's not it. I remember it was just last month. A bunch of people came. They mentioned something about taxes, but I didn't understand. Our manager handled it," Hu Yao said as she continued eating. I noticed a noodle slipping out of her mouth as she spoke.

"Oh, I get it. You're talking about the tax audit. Last month, there was a citywide tax inspection. We wear different uniforms. We're the Market Supervision Bureau, and they're from the Tax Bureau. Gotta get your facts straight," Li Sen said smugly.

"How would I know? The uniforms look the same, and the store was busy at the time. With so many people coming in, some customers left, thinking something bad was happening," Hu Yao replied.

"Alright, let's wrap this up. Li Sen, you take Hu Yao home, and I'll take Xiaoran," I said, finally chiming in.

"Oh, taking Xiaoran home," Li Sen mimicked in a teasing tone. "We get it, we get it. I'll take care of Hu Yao. You guys behave yourselves," he added with a mischievous grin.

I ignored him and quickly finished my plate of stewed intestines. The flavor was incredible. Before long, we had all finished eating. After paying the bill, we parted ways. As we were leaving, Li Sen gave me a strange look, which I understood perfectly well.

Lü Xiaoran and I got into the car. At the time, I was driving a Suzuki Swift—a small car with a manual transmission. She sat in the passenger seat, and as we drove for about a kilometer in awkward silence, I wasn't sure where to go. Most importantly, I didn't even know where she lived.

"I wonder how those two are doing," I finally broke the silence.

"They're probably heading home. Hu Yao lives close by," Lü Xiaoran replied.

"I think Hu Yao might like Li Sen," I continued, trying to keep the conversation going.

"I think so too, but just now, Hu Yao told me she knows that Li Sen is married," Lü Xiaoran said.

"Ah, well, it must be true love then," I muttered, at a loss for words. "How about we go to Yilu Sunshine Hotel?" I asked quietly, so quietly that even I could barely hear myself.

"You mean *Yilu Sunshine Hotel*?" she heard and asked, clarifying. "But I didn't bring my ID," she added.

"No worries, I've got a way," I said, my hands sweating as I gripped the steering wheel, unsure if it was from excitement or nerves.

We soon pulled into the hotel parking lot. I signaled her to sit on the sofa in the lobby and not worry about anything.

I walked straight to the front desk and asked for a room. The young guy at the counter quoted a price, took my ID, and began processing everything without asking any questions. After a few minutes, he handed me the keycard. It was surprisingly easy. I figured he knew what was going on—probably used to seeing people check in like this late at night.

I caught Lü Xiaoran's eye and motioned for her to come over. We walked toward the elevator.

As we entered the elevator, Lü Xiaoran suddenly asked, "Do you often take girls to hotels? You seem to know your way around this."

"Come on, it's not like that. It's late, and you just need one ID to book a room. This is actually my first time taking a girl to a hotel," I said, though even I didn't believe myself.

She didn't reply, just gave me a playful side-eye.

We walked down a long hallway after getting off the elevator. For some reason, our room was further than expected, and the echo of our footsteps filled the corridor.

Finally, we reached the door. I unlocked it, quickly tossed her bag onto the bed, and locked the door behind us.

"What's wrong?" she asked, still surprised by my sudden movements, but before she could react, I lunged toward her and kissed her.

9.Let's sleep. It's late.

Just then, my phone buzzed—the file transfer was complete. As I thought about the events of that night, I caught myself smiling. It had been a night worth remembering, and even now, part of me wished I could go back to that evening. In retrospect, I regretted some of the things I'd said to her that night.

After we had been passionately entangled, I went to take a shower. While in the shower, I hoped she would join me. The idea of us showering together seemed like a beautiful fantasy, but when I finished and came out, she hadn't come in.

She was sitting on the bed, wrapped in a towel, looking distant. Her expression was hard to read, but there was an air of sadness about her. She had turned her face away from me, avoiding eye contact.

"Why haven't you showered?" I asked.

She barely responded with an "Oh," and then got up and headed to the bathroom. As she left, I noticed some tissues on the bed where she had been sitting. For a moment, I thought to myself, *Did she use these to clean herself up? Why didn't she throw them in the trash? What if they become evidence of something?* At that moment, I was still riding the high of having "won," feeling smug.

But then, something didn't feel right. We had just been on that bed, and because it was so late, the front desk had given us a room with two beds. She had been sitting on the other bed the whole time, and now that I thought about it, the tissues were probably from her wiping away tears. She must've been crying.

A little while later, she came out, still wrapped in the towel.

I asked her, "What's wrong? You seem upset all of a sudden. Did I do something wrong?"

"No, I just... I just..." she trailed off, her words broken.

"Just what? Speak clearly," I said, my tone more harsh than I intended.

She didn't say anything else, just looked at me for a moment before turning her head away again.

I can't recall exactly what else we said after that, but I remember that we eventually stopped talking altogether. We sat in silence for a while, and then she finally said, "Let's sleep. It's late."

As I recalled this moment, a chill ran down my spine. Even though it was nearly 30 degrees outside on a summer night in Sichuan, I felt a coldness in my heart. I wished, like in the movies, I could go back and change things.

At the time, I didn't understand what she meant. It wasn't until years later that I realized why she had cried that night. I was only the second man she had ever been with, and she was afraid I would think she was too easy. She feared I wouldn't take her seriously or that our relationship wouldn't last. She didn't know how to refuse me in that moment, but her gut instinct had been right all along.

I put the old phone and charging cable back into the drawer. Who knows when I'll open it again. Perhaps the phone, too, is patiently waiting for its fate, willing to wait however long it takes.

I lay in bed, scrolling through more of the photos Lü Xiaoran had sent me over the years. From the other room, I could faintly hear the sound of Chen Yili's keyboard clacking away. In the quiet of the night, the noise seemed especially loud and irritating. But it also served as a signal—at least she wouldn't be coming to interrupt me while I looked at the photos.

I came across another picture, taken not long after that night. It was from another gathering of the four of us. This time, it wasn't a group photo, but just one of Lü Xiaoran. She was standing next to me, the background filled with other people, yet she stood out in the photo, strikingly clear. She had her head tilted slightly upward, making a funny face, her eyes closed, cheeks puffed out, and hands on her hips.

As I looked at the picture, a smile crept across my face again, but tears welled up in my eyes. In that moment, it felt like I had traveled back to that night, and I could almost hear our conversation.

"Next month's National Day holiday is coming up. I bet we'll have to work overtime. What about you, Xiaoran?" Hu Yao asked.

"Same here. No shifts off for the first three days—we're all working," Lü Xiaoran replied.

"Haha, I get seven days off, seven whole days!" Li Sen boasted, repeating himself several times for effect.

"Well, look at you, living off the government!" I teased.

"Wow, a civil servant, huh?" Hu Yao added, sounding somewhat envious.

"We're not the same as you common folk. He's up in the celestial realm, while we're stuck down here," Lü Xiaoran quipped sarcastically.

Li Sen had certainly stepped into a minefield. Throughout the entire meal, no matter what the topic, we found a way to poke fun at him.

The two girls went to the restroom at one point, and Li Sen turned to me and asked, "So, did you seal the deal that night?"

In our private code, "seal the deal" meant whether or not I had succeeded with a girl.

"Of course," I replied confidently and proudly.

"Nice work. She's a good one. You could consider something long-term," Li Sen said, and for a moment, he didn't sound like his usual self.

"So, how about you? You've got a tougher challenge, right?" I asked him.

"I think it's pretty much done. But hey, it's just for fun. As long as everyone's happy, that's what matters," Li Sen said with a smirk.

The girls returned to the table.

"Should we go sing karaoke afterward?" I asked.

"How about we head over to the Sanxingdui Ruins area? There aren't many people there at night, and you can see fireflies," Hu Yao suggested.

"Fireflies? How enchanting," I said with a mischievous grin.

"Fireflies are just fireflies," Hu Yao tried to clarify.

"We used to have tons of fireflies in the countryside back home," Lü Xiaoran chimed in.

"I'm just asking how enchanting they are," I teased again.

The two girls didn't seem to get what I was hinting at, but when they saw Li Sen smirking, they figured it out. Lü Xiaoran laughed and playfully tried to hit me.

After dinner, the four of us piled into my little Suzuki Swift. I used to complain that the car was too small and cramped, but that night, it felt perfect. In fact, a part of me wished it were even smaller.

"We didn't drink tonight, so how about we take turns driving, Wang? I'll drive halfway, and when I do, you two can sit in the back," Li Sen said, giving me a knowing look in the rearview mirror.

I understood his meaning perfectly. The sneaky bastard. I shifted into first gear, hit the gas, and the car shot forward. Glancing in the rearview mirror, I saw Li Sen use the momentum to pull Hu Yao close, his left hand wrapping around her, while his right hand naturally found its way to her chest.

10. Yeah, you're such a gentleman.

It was about 10 kilometers from the city to the Sanxingdui ruins, far from the museum and close to the original excavation site, an expansive protected area covering tens of square kilometers. Nowadays, access is restricted, but back then, it was an open park, with a main road connecting the various protected sites. Of course, the ruins themselves were closed at night, but aside from the museums, there were still many local residents who hadn't been relocated. This area had a lot of rural businesses, including tea houses and BBQ stands, so even during summer nights, it wasn't exactly deserted.

But our reason for coming here wasn't the BBQ. The main draw was the vast area, plenty of parking, and, most importantly, the darkness. In some spots, once you turned off your car's lights, it was pitch black—so dark you couldn't even see your hand in front of you.

I had already turned onto the narrow road leading into the ruins. There were streetlights where there were shops, but otherwise, it was an endless stretch of darkness.

In the faint glow of the streetlights, I could see in the rearview mirror that Li Sen and Hu Yao were practically glued to each other, kissing passionately.

"Man, those two are going overboard. Are they that into it?" I glanced over at Lü Xiaoran, motioning for her to check out the back seat.

She glanced back, smiled, and said, "You men are all the same. You've got no right to talk."

"I'm different. I don't like being so affectionate in front of others. Feels like putting on a show," I replied, laughing.

"Yes, you're a true gentleman," Lü Xiaoran said with a shake of her head.

We hit a sharp bend, so I braked and downshifted as we rounded the corner. From the back, I heard complaints.

"Can you drive properly? One more turn like that and I'm gonna puke," Hu Yao groaned, clearly feeling carsick.

"Li Sen, your turn. I don't want to hear her whining," I said, pulling over to the side of the road where it was wider.

"Okay, ladies, don't look back here," I joked as I got out of the car.

"What does he mean?" Hu Yao asked.

"Nature's call," Li Sen answered.

The girls were probably speechless at this point. After I came back, we swapped seats. Li Sen took over driving while I sat in the back with Lü Xiaoran, and Hu Yao moved to the front passenger seat.

Li Sen drove more aggressively than I did, revving the engine up to 4000 RPM, the loud sound of the engine filling the car.

"What are you doing? Trying to ruin my car?" I was mid-sentence when my head smacked into the seat in front of me.

It turned out Li Sen had botched the clutch and gas, stalling the car and causing it to jerk forward. The jolt made my head hurt, though thankfully Hu Yao and Lü Xiaoran were fine.

"Your driving skills are amazing," I grumbled sarcastically, just as the car restarted and shot forward again.

Li Sen didn't slow down when taking turns, and the sharp turns pushed me closer to Lü Xiaoran. I used the force of the turns as an excuse to lean into her more and more, until we were practically sharing a seat. However, unlike Li Sen and Hu Yao, we didn't engage in any theatrics. At most, we just held each other.

The rest of the ride was filled with jokes and laughter, loud enough that even outside, someone could probably hear us. The moon was bright that night, and I could see the wind blowing Lü Xiaoran's hair as it flew around her face. She laughed and chatted along with the rest of us, seeming carefree.

It felt like time stood still. The scene froze in my mind, as if we were characters in a movie. I looked at Lü Xiaoran's face, illuminated by the moonlight, as she held onto me with one hand and the seat in front with the other, laughing with Hu Yao. Li Sen had his head half-turned, listening to them talk. Everything felt so real, and I wished for a moment that I could capture it all—if only I had a camera that could travel through time to capture life's most important moments. This would definitely be one of those moments, a perfect snapshot for all four of us.

The scene resumed, and as we drove further, more streetlights appeared in the distance. I watched as the lights passed over Lü Xiaoran's face, one by one, as if the glow was sliding off her.

"Where are the fireflies? Are we there yet?" Li Sen finally asked.

"I think I'm lost. It should be around here somewhere, but maybe we passed it," Hu Yao said, looking around.

"Eh, no big deal. It's not like there's much to see," I said, pretending not to care.

We never did find the spot with the fireflies. As we turned around to head back, we passed a section of road where a few cars were parked.

"They're probably here for some action," I joked to Li Sen.

"Yeah, let's not disturb them. Let's drive by quickly," Li Sen replied.

Suddenly, I felt a sharp pain in my arm. "You must come here often, huh? You seem to know your way around pretty well," Lü Xiaoran said, clearly having smacked me.

"Come on, it's obvious. It's late, and there are no houses around. What else would they be doing?" I tried to defend myself.

"Pull over!" Hu Yao shouted, covering her mouth.

"What's wrong?" Lü Xiaoran, Li Sen, and I asked in unison.

Li Sen immediately stopped the car.

As soon as Hu Yao stepped out, we heard the unmistakable sound of vomiting. She had gotten really carsick.

"Do we have water in the car?" Lü Xiaoran asked, but I had already grabbed a bottle from the back shelf and handed it to her. She got out to help Hu Yao.

"Man, imagine if she'd puked while they were kissing. Would've gone straight into his mouth," I laughed, shouting to Li Sen.

"What are you laughing at? It's late, shouldn't you be sleeping?" Chen Yili's voice suddenly called out.

Damn it, I had actually laughed out loud in real life.

11.So, how about we go to the movies tonight after 9?

I must've dozed off without realizing it. I had no idea when Chen Yili went to bed. Maybe all the memories overwhelmed me and pushed me into a deep sleep.

The next day at work, I immediately called Li Sen.

"Did you know that Lü Xiaoran committed suicide?"

"What? Lü Xiaoran? You're still in touch with her?" Li Sen didn't seem to understand what was going on.

"I ran into Hu Yao yesterday. She told me that Lü Xiaoran passed away six months ago. She died in her rental apartment, and no one found her body for a week," I explained.

"Holy crap, that's horrible. What happened?" Li Sen finally grasped the gravity of the situation.

"How about we meet up tonight?" I suggested.

"Tonight? Hold on, let me check my schedule for this afternoon." I could hear the sound of paper shuffling through the phone as Li Sen checked his agenda. "Alright, that works. I'll be free around 7. Let's meet at

Lao Tang's Beef Noodle shop," he said before hanging up.

At that point, Li Sen had already been transferred to the Deyang Municipal Government Center, so we didn't see each other often. Between our busy schedules and him no longer working in the same city, our meetups had become rare.

Now, I was the team leader of the design group, and most of my job involved assigning tasks and overseeing the team's progress. Occasionally, I'd visit sites too. I opened my work computer and randomly browsed through some of the designs my team was working on. Our data system was shared, so I could view anything once it was saved on the design side. I opened CAD and started tinkering. The first file was a commercial café design. The building's floor plan was filled with too many structural columns, and the designer had used various techniques to make the space more functional and aesthetically pleasing. The floor plan was full of annotations and explanations.

Looking at the complexity of the design, I found myself feeling exceptionally irritable. I kept adjusting the layers, hiding unnecessary guidelines, and leaving only the key structural lines on the screen. I switched between different perspectives, rotating the model to inspect it from all angles, doing the same repetitive tasks over and over. The more I looked, the more frustrated I became. I couldn't focus, so I gave up and pulled out my phone to scroll through my chat history with Lü Xiaoran.

After that night, it seemed like Lü Xiaoran and I hadn't stayed in touch for a while. There were gaps in the messages, and I couldn't figure out why—maybe I had deleted something? Or perhaps the answers would never come.

The next chat was from a few weeks later.

Lü Xiaoran: Was work busy today?
Me: Not really. The National Day holiday is coming up, so things are slowing down.
Lü Xiaoran: Why did it take you so long to reply? Are you avoiding me?
Me: No, I was working on a presentation and didn't check my phone. Don't be so sensitive.
Lü Xiaoran: Oh. So, how about we go to the movies tonight after 9?
Me: Just the two of us? What movie?
Lü Xiaoran: Yeah, just us. It's *Detective Dee and the Mystery of the Phantom Flame.*
Me: Oh, I've heard of that one. Sure, I'll pick you up. Are we having dinner together?
Lü Xiaoran: I can't make dinner. The store's busy today, and I have to work overtime until 8:30, even though I was supposed to finish at 3.
Me: Alright, I'll see you after work.
Me: I'm nearby now. Let me know when you're done, and I'll come over.
Lü Xiaoran: It'll be a bit longer. I still have some things to finish. How about you go ahead and buy the tickets?
Me: ....

As I read through the messages, I remembered what happened that night.

Around 8 PM, I parked near her store, watching from a distance. I sent her a message saying I was nearby, but she told me to go ahead and buy the tickets. Then she stopped replying. I didn't think too much of it at the time, figuring I'd wait a bit. She probably didn't know exactly where I was.

When her shift ended, I saw her walk out of the store. Just as I was about to call her, I noticed her walking straight toward a parked car. The light from the shop illuminated the person inside—it was Zhao.

She stood by the window, talking to him for a bit, then got into the car. A wave of anger surged through me. I held it back and called her.

"Are you done with work?" My tone was cold.

"Yeah, almost. Did you go to the cinema yet? I'll be there soon," she replied, her voice sounding a bit flustered.

"Do you have something else going on?" I asked, trying to sound casual.

"No... no, just a little something, but I'm almost done. Did you get the tickets yet?" Her voice became more tense.

"What time are we watching? I need to know so I can buy the tickets," I pressed.

"Any time is fine. Just get whatever's the next available show. I'll be there soon," she said quickly before hanging up.

In the background, I could hear someone saying, "Going to see a movie, huh?" It had to be Zhao's voice.

I was furious, but I didn't dare confront them. I waited for another ten minutes or so, watching them talk through the car window, though I couldn't make out their expressions. Eventually, I decided to stick to the plan and head to the cinema.

When I got there, I saw that the next showing of *Detective Dee* was at 10:15 PM, the last screening of the night. It was only a little after 9, so I bought the tickets and waited in the lobby for her.

By 9:30, she still hadn't shown up, so I started messaging her.

21:30 Me: Where are you? The movie's at 10:15.
21:43 Me: What's going on?
21:59 Me: What do you mean? If you're not coming, just tell me so I don't waste my time.
22:02 Lü Xiaoran: I'm on my way.
22:09 Me: You're on your way? Where are you?
22:17 Me: The movie has already started.

I didn't send her any more messages. I turned and left. The cinema was in a building at the far end of a pedestrian street, and by the time I reached the exit, the elevators had already shut down for the night. I had to walk down four flights of stairs.

The second floor connected to a sky bridge over the
street, and I planned to take it to reach the parking lot.
As I crossed the bridge, I saw someone running ahead.
As they got closer, I realized it was Lü Xiaoran. The
sound of her bag's trinkets jingling matched the rhythm
of her footsteps. When she saw me, her expression
shifted to one of surprise, mixed with awkwardness.

"Why are you here? Didn't the movie already start?"
she asked, panting.

I didn't respond. I walked past her as if I didn't know
who she was.

12.Out of breath from running, and this is the look you give me?

She stood there frozen for a few seconds, then quickly ran up to me and grabbed my arm.

"What are you doing?" Her voice was urgent and breathless.

I still didn't say anything and tried to pull away, continuing to walk.

"I was just a little late, don't be like this," she raised her voice.

"And where were you just now?" My tone was icy.

"I was busy at the store. There were too many people, and I didn't have time to reply," she said.

"Then we have nothing left to talk about," I said as I continued to walk away.

"Hey, are you really going to act all weird again? Do I need to 'snap you out of it' again?" She tried to get closer to me.

"You're really good at pretending." I only muttered a few words, taking a few steps back.

"Pretending? I ran all the way here because I couldn't get a cab, and this is how you act after I'm out of breath?" she exclaimed.

"Alright, let me ask you, what time did you finish work?" I looked her straight in the eye.

"I was supposed to finish at 8:30, but there were a lot of customers. When you messaged me, I was still busy. I didn't leave until after 10," she explained.

"You're sure you didn't leave the store until after 10?" I stared directly into her eyes.

"Y-yes," her voice started to falter.

"Sure, you're quite the actress. You actually left work right on time. I was across the street, watching you leave the store and get into Zhao's car. Yet, you told me you finished work at 10. I really wanted to believe there was nothing between you and Zhao anymore, but part of you has always been off-limits to me. I can't see into that part of you."

After saying this, I turned and walked away. Lü Xiaoran didn't try to stop me, nor did she say another word. As I reached the corner and turned, out of the corner of my eye, I could see her still standing there, watching me leave. I imagined she must have been crying by now, watching my silhouette disappear into the darkness.

"Peng, I need your signature here," my colleague Xiao Li's voice pulled me back to reality. I quickly rubbed my eyes with my hand and covered them with my palm.

"Ugh, my back is killing me from sitting, and my eyes are strained. Give me a minute to stretch." I wiped my eyes and pretended to stretch to hide the fact that there were tears in them.

"Okay, a few designs are finalized, and the renderings are done. We just need you to sign off on them in the system so we can move forward," she said.

"Alright, I'll check them now and process them."

"Okay, I'll leave you to it," Xiao Li said, sensing something was off but not pressing further, and left.

I logged into the company's online system and found the designs that needed immediate attention. The first one was for a professional esports café, a project I'd been overseeing for a while, with countless revisions before the client was finally satisfied. As soon as I opened the renderings and floor plans, I spotted errors. The dimensions for a four-person station were labeled as only two meters wide. As I kept reviewing, I found even more small mistakes—some items were misplaced, and the entire rendering was unusable. There was no way this would meet the client's standards. I checked the designer's name—Wu Houlin. I cursed silently, *This idiot again.*

"Xiao Li, call Wu Houlin for me," I shouted, louder than I intended.

"Oh, okay," Xiao Li responded.

A few moments later, Wu Houlin appeared before me.

"Did you not check the renderings before submitting them? A four-person station only two meters wide? What, are they supposed to stack on top of each other?" My tone was sharp.

"There are mistakes all over. This client is incredibly picky, and they won't tolerate a single error. If we lose this client, all your hard work is for nothing." By this point, I was practically shouting.

Wu Houlin stood there in shock, not expecting me to explode like this. I rarely lost my temper, especially over something that could easily be fixed with a few adjustments and a new render. But the truth was, my emotions were still raw from everything with Lü Xiaoran.

"Fix it immediately. Stay late if you have to, but get it done," I barked, my voice still raised.

Wu Houlin wasn't a particularly popular figure in the office. He was cocky because his dad owned the commercial building we worked in, and they'd reduced the rent in exchange for giving him a job. Behind his back, everyone joked that his paycheck came from his father.

By the time the workday ended, he still hadn't finished
the revisions. I didn't care to stick around any longer,
so I told him to upload the corrected files to the system
for me to approve remotely. I added that he couldn't go
home until the job was done.

Just then, my phone rang—it was Chen Yili.

"Are you coming home for dinner tonight?" she asked.

"Oh, I forgot to tell you. I'm having dinner with Li Sen
tonight. I'll be back later," I replied, realizing I hadn't
mentioned my plans to her.

"Alright, be home soon," she said before hanging up.

At the same time, another call came in—it was Li Sen.

"When are you heading out? I got back early today,
and I'll be in the city in about 20 minutes. Estimate your
time, and we'll meet at the noodle shop."

"Great, I'm almost done here. I'll pack up and leave
shortly," I replied.

13.She's already disappeared into the crowd.

The evening rush hour in the city had the streets clogged with traffic. Lao Tang's Beef Noodle Shop, in particular, was in an area where parking was nearly impossible. The place was situated in a densely populated neighborhood with street-facing storefronts, and the parking spots along the street were always full. Finding a spot at this time was a near-impossible task.

I had no choice but to park several hundred meters away in a public parking lot. As I walked over, I saw Li Sen approaching from the opposite direction. I didn't need to ask to know that he too had to park far away and walk.

"Been busy lately?" I asked, breaking the silence.

"Not too bad, not much going on," he replied.

As we continued chatting, we walked into Lao Tang's. The place was packed, with several people standing around, waiting for seats. Waves of hot steam came from the kitchen area, hitting us in the face.

"It's too hot in here. Let's wait outside," Li Sen suggested.

We stepped out to wait by the door. Fortunately, noodles were fast food, and seats opened up relatively quickly.

"Two bowls, two liang of noodles," I called out loudly to the owner. The place was so noisy that if you didn't shout, they wouldn't hear you.

"Lü Xiaoran..." Li Sen started to say something, but all I caught was her name before the rest was drowned out by the noise. I signaled for him to hold off and save it for after we finished eating.

Eating noodles in Sichuan's summer heat, especially in a bustling place like this, was a challenge. First, the weather was hot, and second, the kitchen was indoors, so even with air conditioning and multiple fans, it was still stifling. By the time we finished eating, both of us were drenched in sweat, as if we had taken a shower without using a towel. Li Sen's sweat was literally dripping from his hair.

Afterward, we found a nearby café to sit down in.

"It's so cool in here," Li Sen said, wiping his face with a napkin.

"Last night, I ran into Hu Yao at the night market. At first, I didn't even recognize her. It's like she's had plastic surgery or something," I said.

"There are so many people getting plastic surgery these days. I haven't seen her in at least five years, and we haven't been in touch," Li Sen replied, seemingly unfazed.

"I asked her if she had seen Lü Xiaoran recently. That's when she told me Lü Xiaoran committed suicide six months ago."

"Wow... That's intense. Why would she do that?" Li Sen was taken aback.

"I asked Hu Yao the same thing. She said it was over a man, but she didn't know the full details. Apparently, the guy didn't take any responsibility for it in the end," I shook my head as I spoke.

"Was it that Zhao guy? I heard he got into some legal trouble a few years back," Li Sen asked.

"No, it wasn't Zhao. Lü Xiaoran started working at a cosmetic clinic in Chengdu a few years ago, and I think that's when she met this man."

"You two were still in contact? I thought you said you'd lost touch," Li Sen asked, puzzled.

"Not exactly. We stayed in touch on and off, sporadically," I replied, my words a bit jumbled.

As I looked out the window, chatting with Li Sen, my mind drifted back to the memories.

After that night on the pedestrian bridge outside the cinema, we lost contact. In my memory, it had been at least a couple of years since we last spoke.

One evening, I was walking to a department store in Guanghan called BAIHUO Building. To get there from the city center, I had to cross several main roads.

At the crosswalk, the foot traffic was heavy, with people waiting for the green light to cross. As I stood at the curb, waiting for the light to change, a familiar figure appeared across the street, standing on the other side of the intersection, also waiting for the light.

It was Lü Xiaoran.

It had been two or three years since we parted ways on the pedestrian bridge. This was the first time I had seen her since then.

She was wearing a white T-shirt, light blue jeans, and sneakers, standing arm-in-arm with a female friend. The cars passed between us, their lights flickering on her face as they drove by.

She noticed me too. We locked eyes, both of us clearly surprised. Her expression was conflicted—she seemed like she wanted to say hello but was unsure if I'd respond. Her face was a mixture of emotions.

I smiled at her, and she smiled back—a brief, shallow smile. In that moment, the world around us seemed to blur, as though everything else faded into the background. She was the only thing in focus, the singular point in the lens of my vision.

Then, the traffic light turned green. The cars stopped, and we began to walk toward each other, crossing from opposite sides. Our steps were in sync, and for a brief moment, our shadows intertwined beneath the streetlights. Yet, neither of us said a word, nor did we gesture. Our pace seemed to slow as if we were both hesitating, but neither of us stopped. We passed each other without a single word, leaving only a faint trace of presence in the air that was quickly swept away by the crowd behind us.

Once I reached the other side, I turned to look back, but she had already disappeared into the sea of people.

14.How have you been? I haven't seen you in a long time.

"Sigh, karma really comes for everyone. Isn't this what they call a fated entanglement? Aren't you afraid she'll come back as a ghost to haunt you?" Li Sen asked.

"She didn't commit suicide because of me! I didn't even know what was going on!" I spread my hands, trying to show my helplessness.

"I know you genuinely liked her back then. So, what happened afterward? I never knew how things turned out between you two. Tell me the rest of the story. Maybe I can turn it into a script for a short film," Li Sen said.

Li Sen was actually into creating videos and sometimes uploaded them, though they didn't gain much attention. He always complained about not having good material to work with. He thought Lü Xiaoran's story could be a great one, and with some adaptation, it might resonate with people. Honestly, I think that everyone's experiences are somewhat similar, and people often project their own lives onto stories like this.

"So, what happened afterward..." I continued.

After that brief encounter on the sidewalk, our lives went back to having no contact for a long time.

It was the end of 2015. I went to the DMV to get my car inspected for its annual check. The moment you arrive at the entrance, these "brokers" who offer to handle everything for you swarm around. They save you a lot of time, sometimes getting everything done within a few hours. I agreed on a price, handed over my documents and insurance info to the broker, and went to wait in the hall.

Sometimes life has a funny way of bringing people together by coincidence. Some people you may never meet again, while others you're bound to run into at some point.

I had been sitting in the waiting hall for a while, mindlessly reading the news and playing games on my phone. When I turned my head, I noticed Lü Xiaoran sitting in the last row. She happened to look up at the same moment and saw me.

This time, I didn't wait. I got up and walked straight over to her, sitting down beside her.

"What a coincidence, you're here too," I said.

"Yeah, I bought my car in Chengdu, so it's got a Sichuan A license plate. Handling violations can be a hassle, so I came today to transfer the registration back to Guanghan. What about you? What are you here for?" Her voice was familiar, yet somehow distant.

"My car's due for its annual inspection. I handed everything to a broker and now I'm just waiting."

"How have you been? I haven't seen you in a long time," she asked.

"Same old routine—work, then home. What about you? I remember seeing you near the department store last time."

"I remember. I wanted to say hi, but you looked so cold, so I just left," she said, smiling this time.

"No way, I smiled at you. But then you walked away, and I watched you leave," I replied.

"Smile? You were practically scowling, like I owed you money or something," Lü Xiaoran returned to her old expressions and mannerisms.

"I swear, I even tried to follow you, but you disappeared," I said.

"I don't believe you. I stood across the street and looked back toward you, and there was no one there," she said, surprised that she had also looked back toward me.

"So, where have you been working these past few years? Not in Guanghan, right?" I asked.

"I've been to a lot of places. After leaving the jewelry shop, I joined an event planning company. We traveled a lot for work, sometimes within the province,

sometimes outside of it. I wasn't in Guanghan much,"
she explained.

"So, I'd have to make an appointment to meet you?" I
teased.

"You're such a joker. It's not that dramatic. I actually
quit my job recently. I've been feeling unwell and
decided to take a break at home for a while."

"Not feeling well... Are you pregnant?" I joked, and she
lightly hit me.

"No, you're the one who's pregnant! I've just had
stomach issues," she replied, annoyed, but in that
familiar way.

"So, can I ask you out sometime?"

"If I'm free, sure," she replied, but quickly added, "Do
you still keep in touch with them?"

"Who? Li Sen and Hu Yao? I'm not sure if they're still
together. We don't see each other much these days,
and it's not something I feel comfortable asking about,"
I answered.

"Hu Yao has already left Guanghan. She's working in
Chengdu now. They probably didn't continue their
relationship because Hu Yao is getting married."

"Are you married yet?" I asked cautiously.

"No, but I have a boyfriend." The moment she said "boyfriend," I felt a pang of disappointment and fell silent.

She continued, "But, to be honest, I'm not even sure if we can call it a real relationship. I met him when I was working out of town, and he's from another province, even further away. We only see each other a few times a year, and my family doesn't approve. It feels more like a long-distance phone relationship."

"You mean like pen pals?" I interrupted.

Just then, the announcement in the hall rang out: "Number 0368, please proceed to counter 1."

"That's me," she said, standing up and heading to counter 1.

Watching her walk away, I couldn't help but think, if that night she hadn't met up with Zhao, our lives might have turned out very differently. Who knows? Maybe we would've ended up getting married.

But then again, I knew it wasn't possible. Even though we hadn't seen each other, I occasionally heard things about her. Things weren't as simple as she made them seem. During that time, my impression of her had mostly been negative because she'd dated several other guys. I'd overheard conversations at gatherings where people talked about how easy it was to get involved with her, how little effort it took.

In those situations, I would just keep quiet and listen. I never mentioned that I knew her, which only reinforced the misunderstandings.

Just then, the broker came over to inform me that everything was done. I just needed to sign some paperwork.

I went to a special counter to sign, one that didn't require waiting in line. It didn't take long, and soon I had all my documents back. Glancing over, I saw Lü Xiaoran still at her counter, filling out forms. I didn't tell her I was leaving and quietly walked out of the hall.

As I drove toward the exit, I saw her stepping out of the hall. She called out loudly, "Are you leaving?"

"Yeah, I have something to do. Your phone number hasn't changed, right?" I called back.

"My number changed. Did you change yours? We can add each other on WeChat," she replied.

"My number's the same. Just type in your number, and it'll automatically add me on WeChat." I said as I drove away. But through my rearview mirror, I could see her standing there, watching me leave.

15.You're such a cheapskate.

"So, did you two reconnect on WeChat and make up after that?" Li Sen interjected.

"Not so fast. It turned out she got a new phone and lost my number, so she couldn't add me on WeChat. She never managed to add me, and when I tried adding her old number, it wasn't hers anymore," I explained.

"So, you lost contact again?" Li Sen asked, following up.

"That's what I thought. But then, after about six months, I needed to transfer a file on QQ, and when I opened it, I saw a ton of messages from her. I had forgotten we were still friends on QQ. She had been messaging me, saying she couldn't find my WeChat ID without my phone number, and asking why I hadn't replied. She'd been trying for months, sending messages like 'Are you there?', 'Have you eaten?', and similar stuff." As I told him this, I opened QQ on my phone again.

"That's normal. I haven't opened QQ in years either, hardly use it now. So what happened next?" Li Sen added.

"You really love hearing stories, don't you?" I teased.

Of course, after that, Lü Xiaoran and I reconnected on WeChat. How can I describe that time period?

The sidewalk encounter was a turning point. Before that, I still held onto the feelings I had for her, and seeing her again after a few years left me with a lot of mixed emotions. But after hearing all the rumors about her, my impression of her changed significantly.

When we ran into each other again at the DMV, my attitude was different. I didn't take her as seriously anymore, but despite my coldness, she kept reaching out to me. No matter how indifferent I was, she remained positive and persistent.

By this time, the social atmosphere had started to shift. Dating apps were becoming popular, making it easier for men and women to connect. I even heard stories of married women being convinced to meet up with strangers from dating apps for casual flings.

A lot of these incidents happened with one or both parties still being married. Before, if something like this happened, it was usually with someone they knew, like a friend from Mahjong or a gym acquaintance—rare occurrences. But now, dating apps connected complete strangers from all over, providing a fast track for lonely men and women, regardless of their marital status.

I started seeing more of these situations around me. A friend who worked for a large company once joked that the company's social web was like a massive sheet of paper. Once someone poked a hole through it, they'd see an intricate web of connections between people, like a city's subway map. He explained it with numbers: men as odd numbers, women as even numbers. He gave an example:

1—2—4—3—1—4

At first, I wanted to argue, wondering why there were even numbers paired with other even numbers, and why some numbers repeated. But then I quickly realized what he meant and thought to myself, *This is a real mess.*

"Yeah, back when dating apps first came out, they had this feature where you could find people nearby. Women back then were so naïve and easy to trick, and it didn't even cost much. Things are different now," Li Sen chimed in.

"What? Did you have a good run back then, tricking women? How many did you hook up with?" I asked, curious.

"What do you take me for? I wouldn't dare. Do you remember Huang Yi?" Li Sen asked.

I nodded.

"Now *he* was the real master. He got blackmailed for a few thousand after having a nude chat with someone online. Later, his wife found out about his multiple affairs, caused a big scene at his workplace, and he ended up with the nickname 'Public Penis.' He lost his job and now runs a hotpot restaurant, which is doing okay," Li Sen explained.

"He's quite something. I've heard a few stories about him. Where's his hotpot place? Maybe we can go sometime. After all, we were classmates back then," I said.

"Sure, let's go one day. I'll bring my wife, and you can bring Chen Yili. But, ugh, it's people like him that make things worse. Back then, the scene was good—everyone understood the game. You had your fun, they had theirs, and it was mutual. But some guys started using scams like 'pig butchering schemes' or blackmailing people with nudes. These days, trying to randomly hook up with a girl on an app is as hard as going to the moon. You're more likely to get scammed yourself," Li Sen said bitterly, clearly frustrated with how things had changed. I wasn't sure why he was so upset, and I didn't dare ask.

"Alright, alright, let's get back to the story with Lü Xiaoran," Li Sen prompted.

At that time, I was busy with work. I had just joined a new company, and besides drawing designs, I had to visit job sites and meet clients. I also spent time at the big building material markets, negotiating deals and comparing prices. This was during a period when designers made extra income through material commissions, which was a significant boost to my salary.

Lü Xiaoran would frequently message me, but I rarely replied.

At that time, I hadn't met Chen Yili yet, but I had gone through a few quick relationships. They were what you might call "fast-food romances." I'd meet someone at a party or gathering, and before long, we'd end up sleeping together. Just as quickly, we'd lose touch again. It felt random and unfulfilling, and it didn't change the fact that I still lived with my parents, so bringing anyone home was out of the question.

One time, Lü Xiaoran messaged me saying she'd be staying home for a while because her stomach problems had flared up again. It wasn't serious, but she was resting.

Lü Xiaoran: Can you help me pay for something on Taobao?
Lü Xiaoran: Please?
Lü Xiaoran: Hmph, you're such a cheapskate.
Lü Xiaoran: Any plans for tonight? Want to grab some BBQ?
Me: Didn't you say you have a stomach issue? BBQ's not great for that.
Lü Xiaoran: Just because I have a stomach issue doesn't mean I can't eat.
Me: I'll get in touch later, still finishing up some work.

Whenever she asked me to pay for something on Taobao, I'd deliberately ignore it, pretending not to see the message. It wasn't even about the money—usually just a few dozen yuan, maybe a hundred at most. But now, looking back, I regret not paying for a few of those things. Maybe it would've made her feel like someone cared about her. Maybe if I'd been a little more generous, she wouldn't have moved to Chengdu for work, and everything that happened later could've been avoided. Even the smallest change could've led to a very different future.

"You've been watching too many *butterfly effect* movies. What's next, saying a butterfly flapping its wings in Guanghan could cause a storm in Shanghai? Come on, let's stick to the story. Keep going before I have to head out—my wife's going to start calling soon if I don't get back," Li Sen said impatiently.

16.Too bad I never went to college, I wonder what it's like.

That evening, after work, I went to pick her up at her apartment complex. It was in the western part of Guanghan, in an older, relocated neighborhood that looked cramped and worn out.

I parked on the side of the road and sent her a message.

Me: I'm at the entrance. Come down quickly.
Lü: Okay, just changing my clothes.

She had been staying at home for days, probably always in her pajamas. Interestingly, her parents seemed to be quite understanding. Even though she wasn't working, they never scolded her for lounging around the house, which wasn't common for parents of our generation. Occasionally, in our conversations, she'd mention her parents, and it seemed like their relationship wasn't very close, but I never dug deeper into it.

"Let's go," she said as she got into the car.

"Where to?" I asked.

"Barbecue! I know a great place, but it's a bit far, in XINPING Town," she replied.

"What kind of barbecue is so good that it's worth driving over 20 kilometers for? It's almost 8 PM. Are they still open?" I wasn't too keen on driving that far.

"Oh, it's still early. Come on, the food's really good," she said, playfully clinging to my arm.

I've never been able to resist a woman acting like that, so I started the car and headed toward the place she mentioned. The drive wasn't as far as I'd imagined. Once we left the city, the roads were clear, and we reached the destination quickly.

Coincidentally, there was road maintenance going on, and one lane of the road was closed for construction, allowing only one-way traffic. We circled around twice trying to find the restaurant. Finally, we spotted it, but it was hidden behind a blue tent, likely set up to keep out the dust from the roadwork. We had to enter through the side.

The place was near a university, and the restaurant was packed, mostly with college students, their faces full of youthful innocence, laughing and enjoying their barbecue. I couldn't help but think how lucky they were—life was full of possibilities for them.

"What's wrong? Still longing for college girls?" Lü Xiaoran teased, noticing I was staring at the students.

"No, I'm not that pathetic. I was just thinking how this is probably the happiest time of their lives—no real pressures, just eating, drinking, and having fun. Once they graduate, they'll find out how hard life hits," I replied. As I spoke, Lü Xiaoran reached over and held my hand.

"Too bad I never went to college, I don't know what it's like. But I'm still getting beaten down by life," Lü Xiaoran said, her tone a bit sad.

Hearing her words, I couldn't help but squeeze her hand a little tighter. She just smiled in response.

In that moment, I felt like I was watching the memory unfold as a bystander. From a third-person perspective, I stood next to my younger self and Lü Xiaoran. The scene froze: the two of us sitting on the same side of a rectangular table on a long bench in the dim light of the barbecue joint. The soft glow from the lamps created shifting shadows that played across us. Lü Xiaoran was leaning slightly toward me, her left hand holding my right, her face adorned with a sweet smile, while I gazed thoughtfully at the other customers.

It's hard to guess what Lü Xiaoran was really thinking at that moment, but at least she seemed happy. My viewpoint circled around the two of us, like a camera capturing the scene. I wanted to reach out and grab hold of the image, but it shattered like broken glass, except it wasn't glass—it was more like pixels, breaking apart piece by piece. Memories are just fragments, constantly pieced together.

There were no photos from this moment, only these memories. This was one of the few times we ate out together, just the two of us.

"What do you two want to eat? You'll have to go pick out your food from the shelf in the back," the owner of the barbecue joint called out from across the room.

Lü Xiaoran responded and asked me what I wanted. I said whatever, and told her to pick. She got up and went to the back where there was a shelf full of half-prepared skewers, ready for grilling.

I watched as she came back with a large bunch of skewers—beef, chicken, and some vegetables. All standard barbecue fare. She handed them over to the owner for grilling.

Before long, the food was served.

"Do you want something to drink? Beer or soft drinks?" the owner asked.

"No beer for me. I'm driving. Do you have mango juice?" I asked.

Lü Xiaoran asked for a Coke, and the owner went to fetch them.

I knew deep down that the barbecue here was nothing special—just average. It wasn't worth the long drive. I had no idea why Lü Xiaoran thought so highly of it.

"Are we going back after this?" I asked.

"Not yet. Or are you planning on taking me somewhere else?" Lü Xiaoran said with a playful grin.

"Well, since we're all the way out here... how about we go 'wild camping'? Wanna go?" I said with a mischievous smile.

"Stop it with your nonsense! I'll hit you again," she said, pretending to slap me. Then she added, "I just remembered—let's go to that old town nearby, Gaopingpu. We can hang out there for a bit."

Her suggestion made my heart skip a beat. I immediately realized there might be something more to this evening.

17.I didn't have the money to buy it, though the ads were tempting.

Gaopingpu Old Town was a well-known unfinished commercial property development. Back then, they had already constructed a large, ancient-style building complex, even including a tall pagoda. Most of the buildings were empty, with only a few storefronts open on the outer streets. For some reason, the development stalled and it became a ghost town of sorts.

It only took us about 10 minutes to drive from the barbecue joint to the old town. When we arrived, the place was brightly lit, which surprised me.

"I thought this place was abandoned? Why is it so lit up?" I asked, puzzled.

"There are still plenty of shops open on the street outside. Inside, though, there's hardly anyone," Lü Xiaoran said, peering out of the window.

After driving through an arched entrance, we found ourselves on a street lined with vendors selling fruit, hotpot joints, and small grocery stores—pretty much everything you'd expect in a small town. I drove around a bit, but couldn't find a convenient parking spot.

I eventually found a small alley that led off the main road. It looked deserted, so I pulled in and parked. There were no streetlights here, and up ahead were rows of empty, unfinished buildings. We parked the car, got out, and began walking.

Without the car's headlights, the darkness was overwhelming. It wasn't pitch black, but the only light came from the distant street, and even that barely helped.

"Why are we parking here? It's so dark," Lü Xiaoran said, trying to grab my hand in the darkness.

"There wasn't any space outside, and it's safer here anyway," I reassured her.

In a minute or two, we made it back to the main street. The storefronts were all open, and there were a few people milling around. This town was close to Gaoping, so most of the customers were locals, not tourists.

Hand in hand, we crossed the main street and reached the tall pagoda. It was an ancient-style tower, standing about 30 meters tall, but the entrance was locked, so we couldn't go inside. We walked around it a few times before sitting down on a nearby bench.

"The people who bought shops here must have lost so much money. They're really out of luck," I said, looking at the empty buildings.

"I have a relative who bought an apartment here. The developer promised them a rental contract, where they'd get a fixed income from the rent. But after a few months, they stopped paying. I'm not sure what the situation is now," Lü Xiaoran replied.

"There are apartments here? Who would buy them?" I asked, surprised.

"Yeah, right where we parked. If you keep walking, you'll see rows of houses. When the project first launched, lots of people bought in, even people from nearby cities," Lü Xiaoran explained, sounding like she knew the area well.

"How do you know so much? Don't tell me your family bought one too?" I teased.

"No, we didn't. But I came along when my relative bought their place. Back then, the offer sounded so good—things like 'one house for three generations' and a ten-year rental contract. The developer promised to run the whole commercial area themselves. Basically, you didn't have to do anything, and they'd pay you rent every month. It seemed like a sure thing. I was tempted too, but I didn't have the money," Lü Xiaoran said with a slightly embarrassed laugh.

"It's a complicated issue. Back then, there were lots of projects like this. Some succeeded, others, like this one, didn't. There are always many factors at play—poor planning, a weak developer, or just bad timing. You can't really judge these things by today's standards. At the time, it must have seemed like a good deal to those buyers," I said, noticing Lü Xiaoran staring at me intently.

"I think you're amazing. The way you explain things so clearly... I really admire you," she said, her tone leaving me a bit stunned. It sounded almost sarcastic, like she was mocking me.

Damn, I had the feeling she was making fun of me.

We sat there for a while before getting up and wandering around again. It was mostly dark, and there wasn't much else to see, so we decided to head back to the car. As we passed by a fruit shop, Lü Xiaoran said she wanted to buy some fruit.

"You could've bought fruit in the city. How do you know it's fresh here?" I asked, not too keen on the idea.

"Don't worry, the fruit here might be better. Plus, it's cheaper. What, are you looking down on rural areas?" she teased.

"No, no, I wouldn't dare. Go ahead and pick what you want. I'll come in and pay later," I said, waving her off.

As I stood outside the fruit shop, watching Lü Xiaoran move between the shelves, carefully selecting different fruits, I realized that we had known each other for six years. She still had the same graceful figure as when I first met her, but her face had changed. The heavy makeup and youthful innocence were gone, replaced by a more mature look.

"Alright, alright, skip the pointless details. Let's get to the part about what happened in the car," Li Sen interrupted, snapping me out of my thoughts.

"How do you know what's about to happen in the car?" I asked, genuinely curious.

"Come on, I know you too well. You parked in that dark alley for a reason, didn't you? So it'd be easier for you to get up to your usual tricks," Li Sen said with a grin.

I stared at him in disbelief for several seconds before finally speaking. "Is that how all your scripts go? Or is that how you trick other girls?"

"It's not like that... Just keep going," Li Sen said, a bit embarrassed now.

18.Don't worry, it won't affect us.

That night, Lü Xiaoran and I returned to the car carrying the fruit we had bought. I put the fruit in the trunk and saw she had already taken the passenger seat. But instead of getting into the driver's seat, I opened the back door and sat in the back.

"What are you doing? Why are you sitting in the back?" Lü Xiaoran asked, confused.

"Come sit back here."

"Why the back? I don't feel like it."

"Come on, I want to hold you. It's hard to do that up front."

Hearing that, she didn't argue anymore. Slowly, she opened the door and got into the back seat. As soon as she shut the door, I pulled her into my arms. Neither of us spoke; we just sat there in silence, holding each other. She stayed perfectly still in my arms.

Almost as if the weather was on our side, it started to rain. And it wasn't just a light drizzle—it was pouring. We were definitely going to be here for a while. Outside, apart from the rhythmic sound of rain hitting the car, there was nothing but endless darkness. Inside the car, the faint glow of the dashboard buttons added to the cozy, almost sleep-inducing atmosphere.

We stayed like that for over ten minutes before I broke the silence. "You mentioned your boyfriend was coming to Guanghan. When's that happening?" I asked, partly because I was worried she might fall asleep.

"He said he's taking some vacation time, but it'll be a few months. He hasn't bought a plane ticket yet," she replied softly, her voice barely above a whisper.

"I'm curious. How do you maintain a relationship like this? You two only see each other once, maybe twice a year, if that. What keeps you going?"

"He's planning to discuss marriage when he comes. My parents want me to get married soon too. I'm not getting any younger," she said, her tone serious.

Her words stirred up some complicated emotions in me. I wasn't sure if it was jealousy, but I couldn't shake the feeling that we wouldn't be seeing each other as much anymore—like something I had was slipping away.

Without thinking, I pulled her closer. She must've sensed my mood because she said, "Don't worry, it won't affect us. He's hardly around."

"This doesn't feel right. I really don't want to end up getting chased down again," I joked, trying to lighten the mood.

"Again? Why do you always make things so complicated? It's been years, and you still haven't changed," she replied, resting her head on my chest as she spoke.

Looking back on what Lü Xiaoran said, it took me years to understand the deeper meaning behind her words. I often overcomplicate things, letting my own assumptions dictate reality, when in fact, the truth is usually much simpler. At the time, I wasn't trying to interfere in her current relationship. But when she was late to meet me at the cinema all those years ago, I didn't take the time to consider her side of the story. She probably had no choice but to see Zhao, with him waiting outside her work. What else could she have done?

As we grow older, our perspectives change. Lü Xiaoran, who was younger than me, seemed to grasp that better than I did.

"Xiaoran, can I ask you something?" I gently shook her.

"Mmm, what is it?" she asked.

"Why are you still with me? After all these years, I don't get it. I haven't given you much—emotionally or materially. Most of the time, I've probably been a negative presence."

"I don't know," she laughed softly. "I just like being with you. I've never forgotten the first time I saw you. That day is burned into my memory—it was my birthday. I remember the details clearly. You were standing in front of the mirror, trying on clothes, but your eyes kept looking over at me and Hu Yao. It left such a strong impression. I thought, "This guy must not have seen a beautiful woman before. He's staring so hard."

"But I've heard you've had a lot of boyfriends since then," I finally asked the question that had been nagging at me.

"Who's been spreading that nonsense? I'll go hit them," she laughed.

"Though, I did run into a few jerks… and yeah, you were one of them. Hahaha!" Her laughter filled the car, echoing in the enclosed space.

After a few moments, she continued, "There weren't that many, honestly. Some were introduced by friends, and a few were blind dates set up by my family. I took each one seriously, but they all seemed to be just messing around. You're the only one I've kept in my heart, and I don't even know why. I keep thinking about that night we spent at the Sanxingdui ruins."

At that moment, a vivid memory came rushing back to me, as if I were standing in the rain again, watching the couple in the car. The raindrops gently tapped against the windows, the world outside blurring into a haze. They seemed oblivious to the storm outside, lost in their own world. The dim glow of the dashboard illuminated their outlines, casting soft, intimate shadows. The rain streaked down the windows, distorting the outside world, but inside the car, the warmth and affection were clear as day. It was as if the rest of the world had disappeared, leaving only the two of them, wrapped in each other's embrace.

And in that moment, in the present, I leaned in and kissed Lü Xiaoran.

19. I'm Ready. Pick Me Up After Work.

By now, there were fewer and fewer people in the café, and a young waitress was standing at a nearby table, not moving.

I thought to myself: Usually, they stay by the front counter, right? What's she doing here? Is she eavesdropping?

"So, what happened next?" Li Sen asked eagerly.

"Nothing. When the rain eased up, I just drove her home," I said, shrugging.

"No way, I don't believe you. There's no way you would've let that chance slip by," Li Sen doubted me.

I gave him a look, signaling him to lower his voice and be mindful of the waitress. "Keep it down. Don't say nonsense."

Li Sen glanced at the waitress and nodded.

"It's about time to go. It's 10 o'clock, and the café's probably closing. That waitress is practically waiting for us to leave," I said to Li Sen.

"We're not closing yet!" the waitress called out from across the room.

Li Sen and I exchanged a look before standing up to leave. I couldn't help but think, she responded so quickly to what we said. She must've been listening to our entire conversation.

As we passed by her, I said, "You'll probably get off early with no more customers, huh?"

After we paid and stepped outside, Li Sen asked me, "So really, nothing happened after that?"

"Of course not. Are all your scripts just porn? You focus too much on those parts and not enough on plot development," I replied, laughing.

"You gotta have both! Who wants to just watch lovey-dovey stuff? You need love and sex. Anyway, let's head home. We'll chat later. I'll write the script and send it to you. I've already thought about who I want to cast in it," Li Sen said.

"If you make money off this, you better share the profits!" I joked, giving him a playful punch on the arm.

Driving home, it started raining again. In Sichuan, summer nights often bring rain showers.

The rain wasn't too heavy, just enough for the automatic wipers to kick in. Raindrops hit the windshield, streaming down in rivulets as the streetlights outside shimmered and flickered through the water. The car lights reflected in the rain, creating a soft blur, like a thousand tiny, colorful lights dancing before my eyes. The wipers moved rhythmically, trying to clear away the haze, but the road ahead remained indistinct. Inside the car, there was only the quiet hum of the engine and the muted solitude, as the outside world, muffled by the rain, felt distant. It was as if I could still hear Lü Xiaoran's laughter echoing from the passenger seat.

Of course, I wasn't going to tell Li Sen what really happened that night. I'd let him imagine it. After that day, my relationship with Lü Xiaoran entered what you'd call a honeymoon phase. We stayed in touch during the workday through phone calls and texts.

We met almost every other day, doing the usual couple stuff—dinners, walks, movies. Sometimes, we'd even drive a hundred kilometers just to try some hyped-up food.

At a red light, I grabbed my phone and scrolled through our WeChat chat history, finding a conversation from our food trip to Leshan.

Lü: I'm ready. Pick me up after work.

Me: Got it. Don't forget to buy protection.

Lü: You buy it yourself, I'm not getting it.

Me: Fine, I won't use any. Hahaha.

Reading it again made me laugh out loud, but also feel a little sad.

It was a Friday, and I didn't have much work that day. We'd already planned this trip earlier in the week, so I picked her up at 5, just after work, and we hit the highway.

The drive from Guanghan to Leshan takes over two hours, mostly on the highway. Lü Xiaoran slept the entire way. Our destination was a famous "internet celebrity" restaurant that served bobo chicken, a local specialty from Leshan. Bobo chicken is essentially a cold version of Sichuan's classic hotpot skewer dish, but the ingredients are cooked beforehand, skewered, and then soaked in cold chili oil for serving.

When we finally got to Leshan, it was already past 7 p.m., and the city was bustling and packed. The restaurant was near a tourist spot, so finding parking was a nightmare, especially with the one-way streets. After circling for half an hour, I finally found a spot, but we still had to walk another ten minutes. By the time we reached the restaurant, there was a long line outside.

Looking up, I saw a sign that said it was owned by some celebrity's dad. I asked how long the wait was, and they told us there were 31 parties ahead of us, with an estimated wait time of two and a half hours. My head was spinning at that point, so we just turned around and left.

After talking it over, we decided to find another bobo chicken place nearby. We were both starving by then.

There were plenty of options in the area, since they were all in the same general location. It stood to reason that the food at these places wouldn't taste that different from the hyped-up place. After all, when restaurants get too busy, they can't always maintain the same food quality. Sometimes, these lesser-known spots end up serving better meals.

At a nearby intersection, we saw bobo chicken restaurants lining both sides of the street, each with a different name. We couldn't help but laugh at how this really was the birthplace of bobo chicken.

20. My Boyfriend Is Coming Soon.

After dinner, Lü Xiaoran held my arm as we slowly walked along the pedestrian path by the Min River. The breeze gently tousled her hair, and she tilted her head slightly, using her hand to fix it while smiling, as if her smile was carried away by the wind. We walked side by side, with the sound of the river and the soft wind forming the background. In my memory, all that remained was her gentle voice and occasional laughter.

Some of those moments have faded over time, but I still remember the cool night breeze and the brief warmth when she leaned in closer. That night, the stars might have been bright or ordinary, but in my recollection, time stood still the moment she turned her head. The wind may have swept away her hair, but it couldn't take away the beauty of that night.

That was the only time we went on a trip together. We thought we'd be able to see the Leshan Giant Buddha by walking along that path, but after walking for a long time, we didn't even catch a glimpse. A local told us that the best view of the Buddha is from a boat in the middle of the river. Even during the day, you can only see the top of the Buddha's head from the riverbank, since it wasn't designed as a sight for those on the shore. It was built to calm the waters, at the confluence of three rivers.

With no other option, we headed back to the car and decided to find a hotel. Using a booking app, we found one nearby, parked, checked in, and went up to the room.

As soon as we got inside, Lü Xiaoran was glued to her phone, replying to messages non-stop. I didn't ask her about it and went to take a shower. When I came out, though, she was gone—just disappeared from the room.

It was already late at night by then. Where could she have gone? I immediately called her.

"Please don't hang up. The person you're calling is on another line," said the automated message. She was on the phone. What kind of mysterious call would make her leave the room to take it?

As I thought about this, I realized I had arrived home. It was completely dark. I wondered why the lights weren't on.

"Lily, Chen yili!" I called out, using the name I usually called my wife.

It seemed like she wasn't home either. What a coincidence—both the past and the present had merged.

I called her.

"Aren't you home?" I asked.

"No, I'm out with Lao Qu and Zhong Lu. We'll be back soon," Chen yili replied, her background filled with the noise of a night market.

"Okay, stay safe. If you need anything, give me a call. It's raining outside, so be careful," I said before hanging up.

Chen yili rarely hung out with friends—she's a workaholic, spending her nights analyzing data. If she was busy at night, I could only imagine how chaotic her days must be.

I opened my laptop and logged into WeChat on the desktop to make browsing through our chat history and photos easier.

I found the conversation from that night.

Me: Where did you go? I can't reach you on the phone.

Me: Where are you? You left without a word.

Me: ?????

That night, after discovering Lü Xiaoran wasn't in the room, I immediately dressed and went out to look for her. She wasn't in the lobby either. I walked around the hotel, trying to find her, but no luck. I kept calling her, but every time, it was the same message saying she was on another call. I even started wondering if she had been kidnapped, but quickly dismissed the idea—who could pull off a kidnapping from a hotel room without making any noise?

I decided to head back to the room, and as I reached the hotel entrance, I finally saw her.

She was standing in the parking lot, phone in hand, talking animatedly, as if she was in the middle of an argument. I didn't approach her, just watched from a distance as she paced back and forth. Her hand gestured wildly in the air while she talked, sometimes clutching her hair, sometimes swinging her arm. Her expression was tense—eyebrows furrowed, shoulders slightly hunched.

After a few minutes, she still hadn't stopped, so I went back to the room, knowing where she was.

About 20 minutes later, I heard the sound of her key card unlocking the door.

"I went out to take a call. My mom called, and I didn't have time to tell you," she said as soon as she walked in.

"Is everything okay?" I asked.

"My boyfriend is coming soon. My parents want us to talk about getting married," she replied softly.

After she said that, we both fell silent. The quiet seemed louder than any words.

That night, our lovemaking was intense, almost as if I had been provoked. I kept asking her, "Out of all your boyfriends, who's the best in bed? Answer me, quick!"

She shouted, "You!"

Even after getting the answer I wanted, I wasn't satisfied. I kept repeating the question, over and over, with her repeating the answer.

Deep down, I knew the real reason I was acting like this: her boyfriend was coming soon, which meant our time was running out. There was a sense of bitterness, a fear of losing something I thought I had. But what really triggered me was the fact that she had suddenly disappeared again. It brought back the psychological scar that Zhao had left behind.

21.You Only Look at Models, Do I Not Look Good in It?

In the weeks following our return from Leshan, it truly felt like a honeymoon phase between me and Lü Xiaoran. I started to believe that I might spend the rest of my life with her. We even went back to Gaopingpu Ancient Town once more, at night again, and parked in the same spot as before.

I scrolled through our chat history:

Lü: What are you up to, dummy?

Me: At work, drafting designs.

Lü: Check out this link, do you think I'd look good in this dress?

Lü: Did you look at it?

Lü: I'm asking you!

Me: Yeah, I looked. I'm not great at judging these things, but the model looks pretty good in it.

Lü: You only know how to look at models! Do I not look good in it?

Me: You look best when you're not wearing anything, hehe.

Lü: Next time I see you, I'll make sure to give you a good beating!

Reading through these messages, it felt like it had just happened, so close yet so distant. Most of our chats were like this—lighthearted banter. After scrolling through dozens of pages, her boyfriend eventually made his appearance as expected.

From what Lü Xiaoran told me, this boyfriend was from Jiangsu, though I'm not sure which city. They met while working at a large outdoor concert. These concerts were often part of a series of events, including some festival-like programs. From what I understood, her company was in charge of the venue, and they often hosted events in remote locations, like grasslands, where usage was higher during summer. The staff would stay and work there for weeks at a time, making it easy for relationships to form.

Lü Xiaoran said that her boyfriend had pursued her initially and was very kind to her. She had no real support while working out of the province, so she agreed to give the relationship a try. She took it seriously, but over time she realized he had violent tendencies. He was possessive and had hit her multiple times. They lived together for a while, and she even thought they might get married. But one time, after a particularly bad incident where he hit her hard, she quit her job and returned to Guanghan.

Of course, her boyfriend followed her to Guanghan. They lived together at her parents' place for a while. The guy really knew how to win her parents over—he brought gifts, did chores without being asked, and was generally very attentive. Her parents loved him, often telling Lü Xiaoran that men like him were hard to find and that she should appreciate him.

However, Lü Xiaoran felt he was two-faced. In front of her parents, he put on a great act, but in private, he was a different person. Eventually, he had to leave for work and wanted her to go with him, but she refused. After much discussion, they agreed to give each other some space.

Now he was back, and they were supposed to discuss marriage. That's why Lü Xiaoran and her mom had argued on the phone that day.

After learning all of this, I told her, "You've had a tough time. Why do you always seem to meet bad guys? Though, I guess I'm one of them too."

"At least you know! You men are all the same," she teased, giving me a light slap. Then she added, "I ended up working for that event planning company because of another jerk. He told me we'd make lots of money working out of province, but he ran off owing money to the boss. That's why you saw me at the department store that day, and soon after, I started working for that company."

"Wow, your life could be turned into a novel," I joked.

After her boyfriend arrived in Guanghan, he stayed with her family. We still kept in touch but had an unspoken rule not to talk when he was around. The guy really knew how to adapt—whether it was a cultural difference or just his personality, he quickly became popular with all the neighbors in her apartment complex. He probably knew more people there than Lü Xiaoran did!

Lü: Still busy?

Me: Nah, just out having drinks with some friends.

Lü: Anyone I know?

Me: Li Sen's coming by after work. Lü: Speaking of Li Sen, I haven't talked to Hu Yao in ages. She's married now.

Me: That's great! Want to marry me too?

Lü: Don't joke like that! I'll take you seriously.

Me: What's wrong? Can't leave the house again today? Is he watching you?

Lü: Watching my ass! He's at the neighborhood mahjong parlor. He's gotten so familiar with everyone there, he knows more neighbors than I do.

Life has a funny way of moving things forward. Around this time, my family had also started arranging blind dates for me.

One afternoon, I met a very elegant woman at a café called Liangmuyan.

"Hi, let me introduce myself. I'm Wang Peng, an interior designer," I said, breaking the ice.

"Nice to meet you. I'm Chen Yili, a data analyst," she replied softly.

22.That's Great, Congratulations!

I kept scrolling through the chat history with Lü Xiaoran, and it was filled with a lot of photos. She loved taking selfies and sending them to me, often in batches. In fact, many of the photos I hadn't even opened before; I usually just looked at the first one. Since WeChat automatically saves space, any images you don't open remain as tiny, blurry thumbnails.

As I lightly scrolled through, her WeChat profile picture appeared on the screen, still so familiar, as if she were smiling at me from the other side. But when I clicked on the photos she had sent before, the screen turned black, showing a "photo has expired" message. It hit me like a punch in the gut. The smiles, those captured moments, were now lost forever—never to be seen again.

Those black screens felt like an uncrossable boundary, a stark reminder that she was gone, and the memories were slipping away, just like those once-clear pictures that now faded into the void. What was once a collection of warm snapshots had become distant, unreachable fragments, leaving only a deep sense of loss.

It seemed that fate wasn't done playing tricks on her, as another challenging situation cropped up for her, while things between me and Chen Yili were progressing rapidly.

Me: Haven't heard from you in days. Are you guys trying to make a baby or something?

Lü: Make a baby? Gross, cut it out. Me: What's wrong?

Lü: He got caught... with another woman. My parents know, too.

Lü Xiaoran's fate was truly hard to describe. Her boyfriend, who spent most of his time playing mahjong at the neighborhood mahjong parlor, ended up having an affair with one of the women there. The woman was a bit older than him and her husband had passed away due to illness. Somehow, they went from being mahjong buddies to sleeping together. One night, when he didn't come home, Lü Xiaoran went to the parlor to find him, and some of the nosy neighbors hinted at where he was.

Lü Xiaoran took her parents and knocked on the woman's door, catching her boyfriend red-handed. The whole building knew about it by the end of the night.

"How could things get so messed up? How does something like this even happen?" I tried to console her over the phone.

"I don't know... I'm just disgusted by him now," she replied.

"So, what are you going to do? Did he leave?" I asked.

"Leave? No, he's been apologizing constantly, claiming that the woman seduced him. He swears nothing happened, and that when we found them, they had just gotten to her place. I asked why his pants were off then, and he couldn't explain. He even went as far as saying she drugged him and that's why he couldn't control himself."

"Does anyone even believe that? Why didn't he say she was a spider demon and wrapped him up in her web? That's absurd," I laughed.

"I swear, it's like my parents are the ones who got drugged. They kept telling me to keep quiet and not make a scene because it would be embarrassing if the neighbors found out. They're still letting that bastard stay in the house," her voice grew louder.

Lü Xiaoran's parents were the kind of people who cared deeply about appearances. Even after something like this, instead of supporting her, they were trying to sweep everything under the rug. They had spent so much time bragging to the neighbors about how their son-in-law was some high-powered project manager with lots of money, here to marry their daughter. Now that this scandal broke, they were desperate to preserve face, not wanting to become the laughingstock of the neighborhood.

In the end, Lü Xiaoran stood her ground and refused to forgive him, forcing the guy to leave. This situation indirectly pushed her to move away from Guanghan and start working in Chengdu, setting her on a path from which she would never return.

Lü: So, how's that blind date you mentioned going?

Me: It's going well. I really like her.

Lü: Oh? What does she do for work?

Me: She works at a tech company. We actually have a lot to talk about. She even took some of the same courses I did in college, so she understands what I'm talking about.

Lü: That's great, congratulations!

Me: What about you? Did that idiot finally leave?

Lü: Yeah, he's gone.

Me: He's not coming back, is he?

Lü: No, he's not. Do you have time to meet up sometime?

Me: Sure, but we'd need to schedule it ahead of time.

Lü: I think I might be leaving soon. I want to get away for a while.

Me: Where are you thinking of going?

Lü: Probably Chengdu. A friend opened a new beauty clinic there and said I could work there.

23. Not Really, Work's Just Been Getting Busier.

Just then, my phone rang. It was Chen Yili.

"The rain's too heavy, I can't get a ride. Can you come pick me up? I'm at Spring Garden," she said, with the sound of rain clearly in the background.

"Got it. I'll be there soon," I quickly replied.

I walked to the window and looked outside. The rain had turned into a torrential downpour, with gusts of wind bending the trees wildly. I hurried out to the underground parking lot, got into my car, and drove out. At the exit, I saw rainwater pouring into the garage's ramp.

As soon as I left the parking lot, the rain covered my windshield completely. Even with the wipers on full speed, visibility was poor. The drive from my place to Spring Garden was about 8 kilometers, so I had to drive slowly and carefully to stay safe.

This heavy rain reminded me of another rainy day when Lü Xiaoran had come back to visit from Chengdu. We'd arranged to meet in the evening, but just as that night, there was a downpour, and she couldn't get a ride, stranded at the train station. I went to pick her up, and when I got to the station's underground tunnel, I spotted her holding a small bag over her head as a makeshift umbrella. When she saw my car, she ran over and jumped in.

"The rain was so bad, the ride I ordered got canceled automatically," she said as she wiped the rain off with some tissues.

"Yeah, it's pretty bad today. Some areas in the city are already flooded. These rideshare drivers are probably avoiding them to stay out of trouble. We'll have to take a detour around the worst spots," I said.

"Really, it's that bad?" She sounded surprised.

In that kind of weather, finding a place to eat without getting soaked would be tricky, and parking would be a hassle. Then I thought of the perfect place—the mall. Plenty of food options, no chance of getting drenched, and easy parking.

We went to Shijia Plaza, parked, and headed inside. After much indecision about what to eat, we settled on KFC. We found a small table for two, ordered some chicken legs and burgers, and sat down across from each other.

"I feel like you've been replying to my messages less lately," I said.

"Not really, work's just been getting busier, you know? I just moved out of the shared dorm into a small apartment," she replied with a smile.

"You rented a place on your own? Isn't that expensive?" I asked.

"Not too bad. A friend helped me find it," she said calmly.

I could already sense the change in Lü Xiaoran. In the past, I'd only reply to about three out of every ten messages she sent, but now the tables had turned— she barely responded to mine. It was clear from our conversations that something had shifted. Ever since she started working in Chengdu, she seemed distant, and her topics of conversation had changed, often involving the beauty industry, which I didn't really understand. To this day, I'm still not sure what exactly she did at that beauty clinic.

That meal was also when I first realized there was someone else in her life. She didn't tell me his name, so I called him "Mr. X." Her decision to move into an apartment was likely his idea, and it was clear their relationship wasn't just a friendship.

"He treats me really well and is really into me. By the way, how's it going with that girlfriend of yours... Chen, um, what's her name again?" she asked with a puzzled expression.

"Chen Yili," I replied.

"Right, how's it going? Are you guys talking about marriage yet?" She leaned in with a playful smile.

"I'm not sure, but it's going okay. We're living together now in that new apartment we bought in the north part of town," I said.

"Wow, living together already? Sounds like you're happy," she said, still dabbing at her rain-soaked hair with a napkin.

"Tell me more about this new boyfriend of yours. You've hardly mentioned him," I pressed.

"Well, there's not much to say. I'm happy with him, but... he's married," she said quietly, almost inaudibly.

"What? Is your love life cursed or something? You just never seem to follow the usual path," I couldn't believe what I was hearing.

She just smiled and stopped talking. We sat in silence for a long time, the only sound being the faint slurping as I drank from my soda.

Looking at the woman sitting across from me, someone who once felt so familiar, I now saw a stranger. Her gaze had changed too—no longer playful like it used to be. Suddenly, the KFC was flooded with high school students in uniforms, probably grabbing a quick dinner before heading back for evening study sessions.

"Look at these girls. They're so cute. I graduated from this school too. I'm so envious of them. Their lives are just beginning, and they have so much to look forward to," Lü Xiaoran said, her eyes distant, as if lost in thought.

I turned to look at the students too. They were full of energy and laughter, carefree and young, huddled in groups to order food and chat about homework and weekend plans. Watching them rush around with trays and scramble for seats made me realize that they were at the start of their lives, with endless possibilities ahead. Lü Xiaoran, in contrast, had already walked down too many paths, her life framed by realities that had already boxed her in. That's why she was looking at them in a daze.

"Check out that kid, already hugging his girlfriend while ordering food. I wasn't that bold in high school," I joked, trying to break the awkward silence.

24. Just Wanted You to Walk With Me.

When I arrived, I saw Chen Yili standing under an umbrella, looking around anxiously. I lightly honked the horn, and she quickly spotted me and ran over.

"It's already 8 PM, and Lao Qu just asked us to go out for barbecue. A few of the girls are meeting up. I've turned them down a few times already, so I couldn't refuse this time," Chen Yili said as she got in the car.

"Yeah, no worries. You should keep up with your social life. You can't stay cooped up at home all the time. It gets too boring."

"I guess, but they like to drink, and I don't. Every time I'm just sitting there, feeling like a third wheel," she said as she wiped the rain from her hair with a tissue.

Suddenly, I had a strange feeling. The same seat, the same gesture, but a different person, a different time. Yet in my mind, I could almost hear Lü Xiaoran's voice: "You're so weird, I'm going to hit you for being weird." Then came her distinct laughter, echoing in my head like a never-ending melody.

Soon, Chen Yili and I were in the elevator, almost home.

"This weekend, we're going to my parents' house, remember? You promised, so don't flake on me," she reminded me.

"Yeah, I remember. I won't back out."

"Achoo!" I sneezed suddenly.

"Are you getting sick?" Chen Yili asked, concerned.

"I don't think so. I've sneezed a few times tonight. Maybe someone's thinking about me," I joked.

"Well, a lot of people are thinking about you," she teased.

That night, we both showered and went to bed. She fell asleep quickly, even letting out a soft snore—I could tell she was exhausted. But I couldn't sleep. My mind kept wandering back to Lü Xiaoran. So many of the things that happened between us were still fresh in my memory; I didn't even need to check our old chat logs to recall them.

After that night in KFC, Lü Xiaoran and I almost lost contact again—or rather, she stopped replying to me. I sent her several messages, but most went unanswered.

Me: What have you been up to?

Me: Are you there?

Me: Are you coming back soon?

Me: Do you even remember me?

Lü: Of course I remember.

I didn't see her again until half a year later, one night during the Chinese New Year holiday. Out of the blue, Lü Xiaoran sent me a message.

Lü: Are you in Guanghan?

Me: Yeah, I'm here.

Lü: Can you come out?

Me: Sure, where to? I'm alone; she's out traveling.

Lü: Come pick me up at my place first.

After I picked up Lü Xiaoran, she said she wanted to go for a walk. I drove us to the Wetland Park. By then, it was already 9:30 PM. Winters in Sichuan are pretty cold, and the park was practically deserted.

I didn't realize at the time that this would be the last time I'd walk with her in Guanghan. Lü Xiaoran seemed different, like someone I no longer knew. She was smiling, but the smile felt forced. That night, she wore a long coat and high heels, and her footsteps echoed loudly as we walked.

"What's up? It's pretty late for a walk, and it's freezing," I said, shivering slightly from the cold.

"I just wanted you to walk with me," she answered absentmindedly.

"So, are we heading to a hotel afterward?" I joked.

"No, I love him too much. I won't be with anyone else."

"Not even me?" I feigned shock.

"No one. Of course, that includes you," she said as she looped her arm through mine and kept walking.

"Seems like you're the one who's fallen hard. Didn't you say he's obsessed with you? Looks like you're the one obsessed with him," I asked, confused.

"I don't know... I just want to be with him for the rest of my life," she replied weakly.

"But doesn't he have a wife? Aren't you just going to get hurt in the end?"

"He promised he'd leave her. But now she's pregnant again," she said, and I could feel her grip tighten around my arm. It was clear she resented the man's wife.

"This is like a movie, isn't it? These plots only happen in the movies, right? Let me predict the ending for you:

His wife has the baby, he feels guilty, and then goes back to his family. And you, the fool, will still be standing here, waiting," I kept rambling.

"No, he promised me. Once the baby is born, he'll divorce her. I just wish she'd have a miscarriage. One of my friends said she could make it happen—either by slipping her something or by hitting her with a car. That way, she'll lose the baby," Lü Xiaoran said, her expression twisting into something unrecognizable.

"What's wrong with you? You know that's a crime, right? Don't forget, you're the one in the wrong here. What if you were in her shoes—pregnant, with some other woman plotting to kill you? What would you do?" I couldn't believe these words were coming out of her mouth.

I had no idea what Mr. X had promised her, but she clearly believed him wholeheartedly and was now trying to make his promises come true on her own. At that moment, I realized she was no longer thinking clearly.

25.Are You There?

After that night, my interactions with Lü Xiaoran through WeChat slightly improved, but we both started messaging less and less, falling into a semi-silent state. I wasn't sure what was going on with her.

She frequently updated her WeChat Moments, and from that, I could tell her life was still running smoothly. She often posted pictures of food and outings, showing off the places she visited. But I really didn't like the endless stream of "chicken soup for the soul" articles she kept sharing. I have no idea who writes that nonsense, but it's all twisted values. Maybe it's this kind of garbage that messed with Lü Xiaoran's mind, making her unstable.

As time passed, her condition worsened, and we even began to argue.

Lü: Are you there?

Me: Yeah, I'm here.

Lü: He hasn't talked to me in so long. I don't even have the will to live anymore.

Me: It's good he's ignoring you. Just end it.

Lü: No, I love him so much. It must be because his wife is pregnant, and that's why he's gone back to her.

Me: Didn't anything I said last time get through to you? You're the third party, don't forget that.

Lü: My friend said I could threaten suicide to scare him. That should work.

Me: Are you insane? His wife is pregnant. They're a family. Who are you?

Lü: I won't give up. He can only love me.

Me: You're full of it. Go be crazy somewhere else and stop bothering me.

Lü: Get lost! You're the worst person of all.

When Lü Xiaoran called me the worst, I couldn't even argue back. Of course, I was just another bad guy she had met among many.

After that, I started finding her increasingly irritating. I seriously wondered if she had lost her mind, and I began to cut down on contact with her. I just couldn't shake the feeling that she was losing touch with reality.

As the year went on, Lü Xiaoran's behavior became even more erratic. She seemed like she had a split personality. Her WeChat Moments would show everything as perfectly normal, but at night, she would send me messages and photos, mostly about how heartbroken she was, saying how many days it had been since Mr. X had spoken to her. Sometimes, she'd send pictures of herself, tears streaming down her face.

To avoid any misunderstandings with Chen Yili, I started muting Lü Xiaoran's messages at night. Sometimes I'd check them the next day, sometimes I wouldn't check at all, and I almost never replied.

From the flood of messages, I could tell Mr. X was still stringing her along. Their relationship was on-and-off. I figured it was because his wife was pregnant. When he felt lonely, he'd seek out Lü Xiaoran for some comfort, feed her a few sweet lies, and then ignore her again. She was like a spinning top, constantly waiting for a promise that would never come true.

By November last year, her situation seemed to improve. Our conversations felt more normal, and she stopped mentioning Mr. X. She even told me they had broken up, which made me genuinely happy for her.

She even talked about introducing some business to my company.

Lü: Can your company handle hospital renovations? Our hospital is about to start a renovation project.

Me: Sure, I can connect you with someone from our business department.

The next day, I went to her hospital with a colleague. I parked the car but didn't go inside. My colleague went in to discuss the project, while Lü Xiaoran and I went for a walk.

We were in Chengdu's 339 shopping area, surrounded by the constant noise of traffic. She wore a blue suit, which I assumed was her work uniform. Her shoulder-length hair framed a face adorned with several earrings. She looked both familiar and distant, with stories hidden in her eyes. We walked slowly, side by side.

"You haven't thought about getting married yet?" Lü Xiaoran asked first.

"Soon, I guess. Why? Since when are you so interested in when I get married?" I replied.

"Of course I want you to be happy," she said, quickening her pace slightly.

"Are you really done with him?" I asked cautiously.

"Yeah, we haven't spoken in twenty days," she said, smiling.

"You're counting the days? Well, it's good you broke it off. I can introduce you to a new rich guy."

"Sure, I'm holding you to that," Lü Xiaoran finally laughed, seeming genuinely happy.

I remember that day vividly. Her expression was calm, yet there was an unspoken distance between us, like something had already been decided, but I hadn't realized it yet. For a moment, I couldn't even recall her last words. I only vaguely remembered us walking along the road for a long time, until I dropped her off and watched her disappear from view.

That was the last time I saw Lü Xiaoran.

26.It's time to have a beautiful sleep.

In the end, our company didn't close the deal with Lü Xiaoran's hospital. But after that, her condition began to deteriorate again, this time severely. She seemed almost manic, messaging me every day with live updates of her soap opera life with Mr. X.

There was even a time when she pretended to take sleeping pills to stage a suicide attempt, all just to scare Mr. X.

Eventually, Mr. X came back, but only to break up with her for good. He told her not to bother him anymore. His wife had forgiven him for the sake of their child, and he just wanted to put an end to everything.

But Lü Xiaoran clearly didn't see it that way. She became like Don Quixote charging at windmills, insisting that Mr. X loved her, and that it was his wife—the windmill—who was blocking their love. She was determined to take down that "windmill."

She continued sending me messages full of extreme statements, and I figured maybe no one else wanted to respond to her anymore. Perhaps, after all these years, I was the only person she could turn to for emotional support.

Finally, on a day when I just couldn't take it anymore, I replied to one of her messages:

Me: "You need to stop acting crazy. It's too much. Stop bothering me."

She sent me a voice message a few seconds long, saying something like, "Don't think you're so important. I don't need you anyway."

That was the last message I ever sent her.

That night, right around midnight, she sent me another video where she was crying, talking about how much pain she was in. I didn't see it until the next day, and again, I chose to ignore it.

Two days later, on December 11th, she posted on her WeChat Moments: "It's time to have a beautiful sleep." That day was also her birthday, and she had made up her mind.

Yes, that day, she chose to end her life by burning charcoal in her rented apartment.

Mr. X never came back.

At that moment, Chen Yili turned over and woke up.

"Why aren't you asleep yet?" she asked, her eyes half-open.

"I was thinking about what gift we should bring when we visit your parents, and how we should talk about our wedding plans," I replied with a smile.

"Really?" she asked, sounding surprised.

I nodded firmly, and she happily drifted back to sleep in my arms.

The End.